The Bachelor of Arts

R. K. Narayan's writing spans the greatest period of change in modern Indian history, from the days of the Raj with *Swami and Friends* (1935), *The Bachelor of Arts* (1937) and *The English Teacher* (1945), to recent years of political unrest – *The Painter of Signs* (1976), *A Tiger for Malgudi* (1983), and *Talkative Man* (1987). He has published numerous collections of short stories, including *Malgudi Days* (1982) and *Under the Banyan Tree* (1985), and several works of non-fiction. His most recent work is *The Grandmother's Tale: Three Novellas* (1993).

ALSO BY R. K. NARAYAN

Fiction

Mr Sampath – The Printer of Malgudi
Waiting for the Mahatma
The Dark Room
The Financial Expert
Swami and Friends
The Guide
The Man-Eater of Malgudi
The Vendor of Sweets
The Painter of Signs
A Tiger for Malgudi
Gods, Demons and Others
The Ramayana
The Mahabharata
The World of Nagaraj

Stories

The Grandmother's Tale: Three Novellas
A Horse and Two Goats
An Astrologer's Day and Other Stories
Lawley Road
Malgudi Days
Under the Banyan Tree and Other Stories

Memoirs

My Days

Travel

My Dateless Diary
The Emerald Route

Essays

Next Saturday
Reluctant Guru

R. K. Narayan

THE BACHELOR OF ARTS

with an introduction by
Graham Greene

VINTAGE

Published by Vintage 2000

2 4 6 8 10 9 7 5 3 1

Copyright © by R. K. Narayan 1937
Introduction copyright © by Graham Greene 1978

This book is sold subject to the condition that it shall not, by way of trade or otherwise, be lent, resold, hired out, or otherwise circulated without the publisher's prior consent in any form of binding or cover other than that in which it is published and without a similar condition including this condition being imposed on the subsequent purchaser

First published in Great Britain in 1937 by Thomas Nelson & Sons Ltd
Reissued by William Heinemann Ltd 1978
Published by Minerva 1993

Vintage
Random House, 20 Vauxhall Bridge Road, London SW1V 2SA

Random House Australia (Pty) Limited
20 Alfred Street, Milsons Point, Sydney
New South Wales 2061, Australia

Random House New Zealand Limited
18 Poland Road, Glenfield,
Auckland 10, New Zealand

Random House (Pty) Limited
Endulini, 5A Jubilee Road, Parktown 2193, South Africa

The Random House Group Limited Reg. No. 954009
www.randomhouse.co.uk

A CIP catalogue record for this book is available from the British Library

ISBN 0 09 928224 0

Papers used by Random House are natural, recyclable products made from wood grown in sustainable forests. The manufacturing processes conform to the environmental regulations of the country of origin

Printed and bound in Great Britain by
CPI Antony Rowe, Eastbourne

INTRODUCTION
by Graham Greene

There are writers – Tolstoy and Henry James to name two – whom we hold in awe, writers – Turgenev and Chekhov – for whom we feel a personal affection, other writers whom we respect – Conrad for example – but who hold us at a long arm's length with their "courtly foreign grace". Narayan (whom I don't hesitate to name in such a context) more than any of them wakes in me a spring of gratitude, for he has offered me a second home. Without him I could never have known what it is like to be Indian. Kipling's India is the romantic playground of the Raj. I am touched nearly to tears by his best story, *Without Benefit of Clergy*, and yet the tears don't actually fall – I cannot believe in his Indian characters and even Kim leaves me sceptical. Kipling romanticises the Indian as much as he romanticises the administrators of Empire. E. M. Forster was funny and tender about his friend the Maharajah of Dewas and severely ironic about the English in India, but India escaped him all the same. He wrote of *A Passage to India:* "I tried to show that India is an unexplainable muddle by introducing an unexplainable muddle." No one could find a second home in Kipling's India or Forster's India.

Perhaps no one can write in depth about a foreign country – he can only write about the effect of that country on his own fellow countrymen, living as exiles, or government servants, or visitors. He can only "touch in" the background of the foreign land. In Kipling and Forster the English are always posturing nobly and absurdly in the foreground; in Narayan's novels, though the Raj still existed during the first dozen years of his literary career, the English characters are peripheral. They are amiable enough (Narayan, unlike Mulk Raj Anand, is hardly touched by politics), but hopelessly unimportant like Professor Brown in *The Bachelor of Arts*. How Kipling would have detested Narayan's books, even that Indian "twang" which lends so much charm to his style.

> ' "Excuse me. I made a vow never to touch alcohol in my life, before my mother," said Chandran. This affected Kailas profoundly. He remained solemn for a moment and said: "Then don't. Mother is a sacred object. It is a commodity whose value we don't realise as long as it is with us. One must lose it to know what a precious possession it is. If I had had my mother I should have studied in a college and become a respectable person. You wouldn't find me here.

After this where do you think I'm going?" "I don't know."

"To the house of a prostitute." He remained reflective for a moment and said with a sigh: "As long as my mother lived she said every minute 'Do this don't do that'. And I remained a good son to her. The moment she died I changed. It is a rare commodity, sir. Mother is a rare commodity." '

The town of Malgudi came into my life some time in the early thirties. I knew nothing then of the author who had recently, I learned later from his autobiography, thrown up a teaching job in a distant town and taken the bus back to his home in Mysore – back to the world of Malgudi – where without premeditation he began his first novel, *Swami and Friends,* without knowing from one day to another what was to happen to his characters next. I too was working, in a flat in Oxford, on a novel called *It's a Battlefield* which I felt already doomed to unpopularity.

"Soon after morning coffee and bath" – it is Narayan in Laxmipuram – "I took my umbrella and started out for a walk. I needed the umbrella to protect my head from the sun. Sometimes I carried a pen and pad and sat down under the shade of a tree at the foot of Chanundi Hill and wrote. Some days I took out a cycle and rode ten miles along the Karapur Forest Road, sat on a wayside culvert, and wrote or brooded over life and literature, watching some peasant ploughing his field, with a canal flowing glitteringly in the sun."

I was struggling at the same time to follow the movements of my characters through the streets of Battersea and Bloomsbury and along the reach of Euston Road. We had both been born under the sign of Libra, so if one believes in astrology, as Narayan, who once supplied me with my horoscope, certainly does, we were destined by the stars to know each other. One day an Indian friend of mine called Purna brought me a rather travelled and weary typescript – a novel written by a friend of his – and I let it lie on my desk for weeks unread until one rainy day . . . I didn't know that it had been rejected by half-a-dozen publishers and that Purna had been told by the author not to return it to Mysore but to weight it with a stone and drop it into the Thames. Anyway Narayan and I had been brought together (I half believe myself in the stars that ruled over an Indian and an English Libra birth). I was able to find a publisher for *Swami*, and Malgudi was born, the Mempe Forest and Nallappa's Grove, the Albert Mission School, Market Road, the River Sarayu – all that region of the imagination which seems to me now more familiar than Battersea or the Euston Road.

In the eleven novels which extend from *Swami and*

Friends to *The Painter of Signs* Narayan has never, I think, strayed far from Malgudi, though a character may sometimes disappear for ever into India, like Rajam, friend of the schoolboy Swami, simply by taking a train. Year by year Narayan has peopled Malgudi with characters we never forget. In his second novel – a very funny and happy book – there is Chandran, little more than a schoolboy, whom we leave at the end of *The Bachelor of Arts* in a bubble of excitement at a marriage which has been arranged with the help of a dubious, even dishonest, horoscope. In his third book, *The English Teacher,* the marriage ends in death and Narayan shows how far he has grown as a writer to encompass the sadness and loss. In *The Dark Room* the screw of unhappiness is twisted further, the killing of love more tragic than the death of love.

Narayan himself had known the death of love, and *The English Teacher* is dedicated to his dead wife. It took some years before a degree of serenity and humour returned to Malgudi with *The Financial Expert* and his "office" under a banyan tree, with Mr Sampath, the over optimistic film producer, the sweet vendor's son Mali and his novel writing machine, Raman, the sign painter who was lured by love of Daisy from his proper work to make propaganda in the countryside for birth control and sterilisation, the bullying taxidermist, Vasu, in *The Man-*

Eater of Malgudi, perhaps Narayan's best comic character.

Something had permanently changed in Narayan after *The Bachelor of Arts*, the writer's personal tragedy has been our gain. Sadness and humour in the later books go hand in hand like twins, inseparable, as they do in the stories of Chekhov. Perhaps if we had read more closely we should have seen that the shadow had been there from the beginning. A writer in some strange way knows his own future – his end is in his beginning, as it is in the pages of a horoscope, and the schoolboy Swami, watching the friend with whom he had needlessly quarrelled, vanish into the vast unknown spaces of India, had already experienced a little of what Krishna came to feel as he watched his beloved wife die of typhoid. One is tempted to exclaim: isn't the imaginative experience enough? Why should the author have had to suffer in himself the agony of his characters?

PART ONE

CHAPTER ONE

§

CHANDRAN was just climbing the steps of the College Union when Natesan, the secretary, sprang on him and said, "You are just the person I was looking for. You remember your old promise?"

"No," said Chandran promptly, to be on the safe side.

"You promised that I could count on you for a debate any time I was hard pressed for a speaker. You must help me now. I can't get a Prime Mover for the debate to-morrow evening. The subject is that in the opinion of this house historians should be slaughtered first. You are the Prime Mover. At five to-morrow evening." He tried to be off, but Chandran caught his hand and held him: "I am a history student. I can't move the subject. What a subject ! My professor will eat me up."

"Don't worry. I won't invite your professor."

"But why not some other subject ?"

"We can't change the Union Calendar now."

Chandran pleaded, "Any other day, any other subject."

"Impossible," said the secretary, and shook himself free.

"At least make me the Prime Opposer," pleaded Chandran.

"You are a brilliant Mover. The notices will be out in an hour. To-morrow evening at five. . . ."

Chandran went home and all night had dreams of picking up a hatchet and attacking his history professor, Ragavachar. He sat down next morning to prepare for the debate. He took out a piece of paper and wrote :

"His'ians to be slaughtered first. Who should come second ? Scientists or carpenters ? Who will make knife-handles if carpenters are killed first ? In any case why kill anybody ? Must introduce one or two humorous stories. There was once a his'ian who dug in his garden and unearthed two ancient coins, which supplied the missing link of some period or other; but lo ! they were not ancient coins after all but only two old buttons. . . . Oh, a most miserable story. Idiotic. What am I to do? Where can I get a book full of jokes of a historical nature? A query in some newspaper. Sir, will you or any of your numerous readers kindly let me know where I can get historical humours?" It was quite an hour before Chandran woke up and his pen ceased. He looked through the jottings that were supposed to be notes for his evening speech. He suddenly realized that his mind wandered when he held pen over paper, but he could concentrate intensely when he walked about with bent head. He considered this a very important piece of self-realization.

He pushed his chair back, put on his coat, and went out. After about two hours of wandering he returned home, having thought of only one argument for killing historians first, namely, that they might not be there to misrepresent the facts when scientists, poets, and statesmen were being killed in their turn. It appeared to him a very brilliant argument. He could see before him a whole house rocking with laughter. . . .

§

Chandran spent a useful half-hour gazing at the college notice board. He saw his name in a notice announcing the evening's debate. He marched along the corridor, with a preoccupied look, to his class. With difficulty he listened to the lecture and took down notes. When the hour closed and the lecturer left the class, Chandran sat back, put the cap on his pen, and let his mind dwell on the subject of historians. He had just begun a short analysis of the subject when Ramu, sitting three benches down the gallery, shouted to him: " Shall we go out for a moment till Brown comes in ? "

" No."

" Why not ? "

Chandran was irritated. " You can go if you like."

" Certainly. And you can just stay there and mope," said Ramu, and walked down the gallery. Chandran felt relieved at his exit, and was settling down to further meditations on historians when somebody asked him to lend his notes of the lecture in the previous hour ; somebody else wanted something else. It went on like that till Professor Brown, principal of the college, entered the class with a pile of books under his arm. This was an important hour, Greek Drama. Chandran had once again to switch his mind off the debate.

At the end of the hour Chandran went to the

library and looked through the catalogue. He opened several shelves and examined the books. He could not get the slightest help or guidance. The subject of the debate seemed to be unique. There was any quantity of literature in support of history, but not one on the extermination of historians.

He went home at three. He had still two hours before the debate. He said to his mother, "I am speaking in a debate this evening. I am now going to my room to prepare. Nobody must knock on my door or shout near my window."

He came out of his room at four-thirty, ran up and down the hall, banged his fists on the bathroom door, splashed cold water on his head, and ran back to his room. He combed and brushed his crop, put on his chocolate-coloured tweed coat, which was reserved for special occasions, and hurried out of the house.

§

Natesan, the secretary, who was waiting with a perspiring face on the Union veranda, led Chandran into the hall and pushed him into his seat—the first of the four cushioned chairs arranged below the platform for the main debaters. Chandran mopped his face with his handkerchief and looked about.

The gallery, built to accommodate about a thousand members of the Union, was certainly not filled to overflowing. There were about fifty from the junior classes and a score from the Final Year classes. Natesan bent over Chandran's shoulder and whispered, "Good house, isn't it?" It was quite a big gathering for a Union debate.

A car stopped outside with a roar. The secretary dashed across the hall and returned in a moment, walking sideways, with a feeble official smile on his face, followed by Professor Brown. He led the professor to the high-backed chair on the platform, and whispered to him that he might open the proceedings. Professor Brown rose and announced, "I call upon Mr. H. V. Chandran to move the proposition . . ." and sat down.

The audience clapped their hands. Chandran rose, looked fixedly at the paperweight on the table, and began, "Mr. Speaker, I am certain that this house, so well known for its sanity and common sense, is going to back me solidly when I say that historians should be slaughtered first. I am a student of History and I ought to know. . . ."

He went on thus for about twenty minutes, inspired by the applause with which the audience received many of his cynicisms.

After that the Prime Opposer held the attention of the audience for about twenty minutes. Chandran noted with slight displeasure that the audience received his speech with equal enthusiasm. And then the seconders of the prime speakers droned on for about ten minutes, each almost repeating what their principals had said. When the speakers in the gallery rose there was an uproar, and Professor Brown had to ring the bell and shout "Order, order." Chandran felt very bored. Now that he had delivered his speech he felt that the speeches of the others in the hall were both unnecessary and inferior. His eyes wandered about the hall. He looked at the Speaker on the platform. He kept gazing at Professor Brown's pink face. Here he is, Chandran thought, pretending to press the bell and listen to the speeches, but really his thoughts are at the tennis court and the card-table in the English Club. He is here not out of love for us, but merely to keep up appearances. All Europeans are like this. They will take their thousand or more a month, but won't do the slightest service to Indians with a sincere heart. They must be paid this heavy amount for spending their time in the English Club. Why should not these fellows admit Indians to their clubs? Sheer colour arrogance. If ever I get into power I shall see that Englishmen attend clubs along with Indians and are not so exclusive. Why not give the poor devils—so far away from their home—a chance to club together at least for a few hours at the end of a day's work? Anyway who invited them here?

Into this solo discussion Professor Brown's voice impinged: "Members from the House having expressed their views, and the Prime Opposer having summed up, I call upon Mr. Chandran to speak before putting the proposition to the vote."

Chandran hurriedly made one or two scratches on a sheet of paper, rose, and began: "Mr. Speaker and the Honourable House, I have followed with keen excitement the views expressed by the honourable members of this House. It has considerably lightened my task as the Prime Mover. I have no doubt what the verdict of this House will be on this proposition. . . ." He spun out sentences till the Speaker rang the bell to stop him. Before sitting down he threw in his anecdote about the professor who dug up brass buttons in his garden.

When the division was taken the House, by an overwhelming majority, voted for an early annihilation of historians. Chandran felt victorious. He dramatically stretched his arm across the table and shook hands with the Prime Opposer.

Professor Brown rose and said that technically he ought not to speak, and then explained for five minutes why historians should be slaughtered and for five minutes why they should be deified. He complimented the movers on their vigorous arguments for the proposition, and the opposers on the able stand they had taken.

As soon as he sat down, the secretary jumped on to the platform and mumbled a vote of thanks. By the time the vote of thanks was over the hall had become empty and silent.

Chandran lingered in the doorway as the lights were dimmed, and the secretary, in a very exhausted condition, supervised the removal of the paper-weights and table-cloth to the store-room.

"You are coming my way?" Chandran asked.

"Yes."

"Well, the meeting is over," said the secretary as they descended the Union steps. Chandran hoped that the secretary would tell him something about his speech. But the secretary was busy with his own thoughts. "I am sorry I ever took up this business," he said. "Hardly any time is left over for my studies. We are already in the middle of August and I don't know what Political Philosophy is."

Chandran was not interested in the travails of a secretary. He wanted him to say something about his own speech in the debate. So he said, "Nobody invited you to become the secretary. You forget that you begged, borrowed, and stole votes at the Union elections."

"I agree with you," the secretary said. "But what is to be done about it now?"

"Resign," said Chandran. He resented the secretary's superficial interest in Chandran's speech. He had cringed for Chandran's help before the debate, and immediately the thing was over did not trouble to make the slightest reference to the speech.

"I will tell you a secret," the secretary said. "If I had kept clear of the Union elections, I should have saved nearly seventy rupees."

"What do you mean?"

"Every vote was purchased with coffee and tiffin, and, in the election month, the restaurant bill came to seventy. My father wrote to me from the village asking if I thought that rupees lay scattered in our village street."

Chandran felt sympathy for him, but was still disappointed that he made no reference to his speech.

There was no use waiting for him to open the subject. He was a born grumbler. Settle all his debts and give him all the comforts in the world, he would still have something to grumble about.

"I have not paid the restaurant bill yet . . ." began the secretary. Chandran ignored this and asked abruptly:

"What do you think of the Boss's speech?"

"As humorous as ever," said the secretary.

"It is an idiotic belief you fellows have that everything he says is humorous. He has only to move his lips for you to hold your sides and laugh."

"Why are you so cynical?"

"I admit he has genuine flashes of humour, but . . ."

"You can't deny that Brown is a fine principal. He has never turned down any request to preside at meetings."

"That is all you seem to care for in a man. Presiding over meetings! It proves nothing."

"No. No. I only mean that he is a very pleasant man."

"He is a humbug, take it from me," said Chandran. "He gets his thousand a month, and no wonder he is pleasant. Remember that he is a scoundrel at heart."

They had now covered half the length of Market

Road. As they passed the fountain in the Square, Chandran realized that he was wasting much time and energy in a futile discussion. A few paces more and they would be at the mouth of Kabir Street. A few more moments of that futile discussion and the other would turn and vanish in the darkness. Chandran resolved to act while there was still time: "Secretary, how did you like my speech to-day?"

The secretary stopped, gripped Chandran's hand and said, "It was a wonderful speech. You should have seen Brown's face as he watched you. He would certainly have clapped his hands, but for the fact that he was the Speaker. . . . I say, I really liked your story about the professor and his buttons. Such a thing is quite possible, you know. Fine speech, fine speech. So few are really gifted with eloquence."

When they came to Kabir Street, Chandran asked sympathetically, "You live here?"

"Yes."

"With your people?"

"They are in the village. I have taken a room in a house where a family lives. I pay a rent of about three rupees. It is a small room."

"Boarding?"

"I go to a hotel. The whole thing comes to about fifteen rupees. Wretched food, and the room is none too good. But what can I do? After the elections my father cut my allowance, and I had to quit the college hostel. Why don't you come to my room some day?"

"Certainly, with pleasure," said Chandran.

"Good-night."

The secretary had gone a few yards down Kabir Street, when Chandran called suddenly, "Here, secretary!" The other came back. Chandran said, "I did not mean that thing about your resignation seriously. Just for fun."

"Oh, it is all right," said the secretary.

"Another thing," said Chandran. "Don't for a moment think that I dislike Brown. I agree with you entirely when you say he is a man with a pleasant manner. He has a first-rate sense of humour. He is a great scholar. It is really a treat to be taught Drama by him. I was only trying to suggest that people saw humour even where he was serious. So please don't mistake me."

"Not at all," said the secretary, and melted in the darkness of Kabir Street.

Chandran had still a quarter of Market Road to walk. A few dim Municipal lamps, and the gas lamps of the roadside shops, lit the way. Chandran walked, thinking of the secretary. The poor idiot ! Seemed to be always in trouble and always grumbling. Probably borrowed a lot. Must be taking things on credit everywhere, in addition to living in a dingy room and eating bad food. What with a miserly father in the village and the secretary's work and one thing and another, how was he to pass his examination ? Not a bad sort. Seemed to be a sensible fellow.

His feet had mechanically led him to Lawley Extension. His was the last bungalow in the Second Cross Road of the Extension. As he came before the house that was the last but one, he stopped and shouted from the road, " Ramu ! "

" Coming ! " a voice answered from inside.

Ramu came out. " Didn't you come to the debate ? " Chandran asked.

" I tried to be there, but my mother wanted me to escort her to the market. How did it go off ? "

" Quite well, I think. The proposition was carried."

" Really ! " Ramu exclaimed, and shook Chandran's hand.

They were as excited as if it were the Finance Bill before the Legislative Assembly in Delhi.

"My speech was not bad," said Chandran. "Brown presided. I was told that he liked it immensely. . . ."

"Good crowd?"

"Fairly good. Two rows of the gallery were full. I am really sorry you were not there."

"How did the others speak?"

"The voting ought to indicate. Brown really made a splendid speech in the end. It was full of the most uproarious humour."

Chandran asked, "Would you care to see a picture to-night?"

"It's nearly nine."

"It doesn't matter. You've finished your dinner. I won't take even five minutes. Put on your coat and come."

Ramu asked, "I hope you are paying for both of us?"

"Of course," said Chandran.

§

As Chandran came to his gate, he saw his father in the veranda, pacing up and down. Late-coming was one of the few things that upset him. Chandran hesitated for a moment before lifting the gate chain.

He opened the gate a little, slipped in, and put the chain back on its hook noiselessly. His usual move after this would be to slip round to the back-door and enter the house without his father's knowledge. But now he had a surge of self-respect. He realized that what he usually did was a piece of evasive cowardice worthy of an adolescent. He was not eighteen but twenty-one. At twenty-one to be afraid of one's parents and adopt sneaky ways! He would be a graduate very soon and he was already a remarkable orator!

This impulse to sneak in was very boyish. He felt sorry for it and remedied it by unnecessarily lifting the gate chain and letting it noisily down. The slightest noise at the gate excited an alert watchfulness in his father. And as his father stood looking towards the gate, Chandran swaggered along the drive with an independent air, but within he had a feeling that he should have chosen some other day for demonstrating his independence. Here he was, later than ever, with a cinema programme before him, and his father would certainly stop him and ask a lot of questions. He mounted the veranda steps. His father said, " It is nine."

" I spoke in a debate, Father. It was late when it closed."

"How did you fare in the debate?"

Chandran gave him an account of it, all the time bothered about the night show. Father never encouraged any one to attend a night show.

"Very good," Father said. "Now get in and have your food. Your mother is waiting."

Chandran, about to go in, said casually, "Father, Ramu will be here in a moment; please ask him to wait."

"All right."

"We are going to a cinema to-night. . . . We are in a rather festive mood after the debate."

"H'm. But I wouldn't advise you to make it a habit. Late shows are very bad for the health."

He was in the dining-room in a moment, sitting before his leaf and shouting to the cook to hurry up.

The cook said, "Please call your mother. She is waiting for you."

"All right. Bring me first rice and curd."

He then gave a shout, "Mother!" which reached her as she sat in the back veranda, turning the prayer beads in her hand, looking at the coconut trees at the far end of the compound. As she turned the beads, her lips uttered the holy name of Sri Rama, part of her mind busied itself with thoughts of her husband, home, children, and relatives, and her eyes took in the delicate beauty of coconut trees waving against a starlit sky.

By the time she reached the dining-room Chandran had finished his dinner. She slowly walked to the *puja* room, hung the string of beads on a nail, prostrated before the gods, and then came to her leaf. By that time Chandran was gone. Mother sat before her leaf and asked the cook, " Didn't he eat well ? "

" No. He took only rice and curd. He bolted it down."

She called Chandran.

" What, Mother ? "

" Why are you in such a hurry ? "

" I am going to the cinema."

" I had that potato sauce prepared specially for you, and you have eaten only curd and rice ! Fine boy ! "

" Mother, give me a rupee."

She took out her key bunch and threw it at him. " Take it from the drawer. Bring the key back."

§

They walked to the cinema. Chandran stopped at a shop to buy some betel leaves and a packet of cigarettes. Attending a night show was not an ordinary affair. Chandran was none of your business-like automatons who go to a cinema, sit there, and return home. It was an æsthetic experience to be approached with due preparation. You must chew the betel leaves and nut, chew gently, until the heart was stimulated and threw out delicate beads of perspiration and caused a fine tingling sensation behind the ears; on top of that you must light a cigarette, inhale the fumes, and with the night breeze blowing on your perspiring forehead, go to the cinema, smoke more cigarettes there, see the picture, and from there go to an hotel nearby for hot coffee at midnight, take some more betel leaves and cigarettes, and go home and sleep. This was the ideal way to set about a night show. Chandran squeezed the maximum æsthetic delight out of the experience, and Ramu's company was most important to him. It was his presence that gave a sense of completion to things. He too smoked, chewed, drank coffee, laughed (he was the greatest laugher in the world), admired Chandran, ragged him, quarrelled with him, breathed delicious scandal over the names of his professors and friends and unknown people.

The show seemed to have already started, because

there was no crowd outside the Select Picture House. It was the only theatre that the town possessed, a long hall roofed with corrugated iron sheets. At the small ticket-window Chandran inquired, " Has the show begun ? "

" Yes, just," said the ticket man, giving the stock reply.

You might be three-quarters of an hour late, yet the man at the ticket window would always say, " Yes, just."

" Hurry up, Ramu," Chandran cried as Ramu slackened his pace to admire a giant poster in the narrow passage leading to the four-annas entrance.

The hall was dark ; the ticket collector at the entrance took their tickets and held apart the curtains. Ramu and Chandran looked in, seeking by the glare of the picture on the screen for vacant seats. There were two seats at the farthest end. They pushed their way across the knees of the people already seated. " Head down ! " somebody shouted from a back seat, as two heads obstructed the screen. Ramu and Chandran stooped into their seats.

It was the last five minutes of a comic in which Jas Jim was featured. That fat genius, wearing a ridiculous cap, was just struggling out of a paint barrel.

Chandran clicked his tongue in despair : " What a pity. I didn't know there was a Jas two-reeler with the picture. We ought to have come earlier."

Ramu sat rapt. He exploded with laughter. " What a genius he is ! " Chandran murmured as Jas got on his feet, wearing the barrel around his waist like a kilt. He walked away from Chandran, but turned once to throw a wink at the spectators, and, taking a step back, stumbled and fell, and rolled off, and the picture ended. A central light was switched on. Chandran and Ramu raised themselves in their seats, craned their necks, and surveyed the hall.

The light went out again, the projector whirred. Scores of voices read aloud in a chorus, " Godfrey T. Memel presents Vivian Troilet and Georgie Lomb in *Lightguns of Lauro* . . ." and then came much unwanted information about the people who wrote the story, adapted it, designed the dresses, cut the film to its proper length, and so on. Then the lyrical opening : " Nestling in the heart of the Mid-West, Lauro city owed its tranquillity to the eagle-eyed sheriff——" ; then a scene showing a country girl (Vivian Troilet) wearing a check skirt, going up a country lane. Thus started, though with a deceptive quietness, it moved at a breathless pace, supplying love, valour, villainy, intrigue, and battle in enormous quantities for a whole hour. The notice " Interval " on the screen, and the lights going up, brought Chandran and Ramu down to the ordinary plane. The air was thick with tobacco smoke. Ramu yawned, stood up, and gazed at the people occupying the more expensive seats behind them. " Chandar, Brown is here with some girl in the First Class."

" May be his wife," Chandran commented without turning.

" It is not his wife."

" Must be some other girl, then. The white fellows are born to enjoy life. Our people really don't know how to live. If a person is seen with a girl by his side, a hundred eyes stare at him and a hundred tongues comment, whereas no European ever goes out without taking a girl with him."

" This is a wretched country," Ramu said with feeling.

At this point Chandran had a fit of politeness. He pulled Ramu down, saying that it was very bad manners to stand up and stare at the people in the back seats.

Lights out again. Some slide advertisements, each lasting a second.

" Good fellow, he gets through these inflictions quickly," said Chandran.

" For each advertisement he gets twenty rupees a month."

" No, it is only fifteen."

" But somebody said that it was twenty."

" It is fifteen rupees. You can take it from me," Chandran said.

" Even then, what a fraud! Not one stays long enough. I hardly take in the full name of that baby's nourishing food, when they tell me what I ought to smoke. Idiots. I hate advertisements."

The advertisements ended and the story started again from where it had been left off. The hero smelt the ambush ten yards ahead. He took a short cut, climbed a rock, and scared the ruffians from behind. And so on and on it went, through fire and water, and in the end the good man Lomb always came out triumphant; he was an upright man, a courageous man, a handsome man, and a strong man, and he had to win in the end. Who could not foresee it? And yet every day at every show the happy end was awaited with breathless suspense. Even the old sheriff (all along opposed to the union of Vivian with Georgie) was suddenly transformed, and with tears in his eyes he placed her hands on his. There was a happy moment before the end, when the lovers' heads were shown on an immense scale, their lips welded in a kiss. Good-night.

Lights on. People poured out of the exits, sleepy, yawning, rubbing their smarting eyes. This was the worst part of the evening, this trudge back home, all the way from the Select Picture House to Lawley Extension. Two or three cars sounded their horns and started from the theatre.

" Lucky rascals. They will be in their beds in five minutes. When I start earning I shall buy a car first of all. Nothing like it. You can just see the picture and go straight to bed."

" Coffee ? " Chandran asked, when they passed a brightly lit coffee hotel.

" I don't much care."

" Nor do I."

They walked in silence for the most part, occasionally exchanging some very dull, languid jokes.

As soon as his house was reached, Ramu muttered, " Good-night. See you to-morrow," and slipped through his gate.

Chandran walked on alone, opened the gate silently, woke up his younger brother sleeping in the hall, had the hall door opened, and fumbled his way to his room. He removed his coat in the dark, flung it on a chair, kicked a roll of bedding on the floor, and dropped down on it and closed his eyes even before the bed had spread out.

CHAPTER TWO

§

JULY, August, September, and October were months that glided past without touching the conscience. One got up in the morning, studied a bit, attended the classes, promenaded the banks of Sarayu River in the evenings, returned home at about eight-thirty, talked a little about things in general with the people at home, and then went to bed. It did not matter whether all the books were on the table or whether the notes of lectures were up-to-date. Day after day was squandered thus till one fine morning the young men opened their eyes and found themselves face to face with November. The first of November was to a young man of normal indifference the first reminder of the final trial—the examination. He now realized that half the college year was already spent. What one ought to do in a full year must now be done in just half the time.

On November the first Chandran left his bed at 5 a.m., bathed in cold water, and sat at his study table, before even his mother, the earliest riser in the house, was up. He sat there strengthening himself with several resolutions. One was that he would get up every day at the same hour, bathe in cold water, and get through three hours of solid work before starting for the college. The second resolution was that he would be back home before eight in the evenings and study till eleven-thirty. He also resolved not to smoke because it was bad for the heart, and a very sound heart was necessary for the examination.

He took out a sheet of paper and noted down all his subjects. He calculated the total number of preparation hours that were available from November the first to March. He had before him over a thousand hours, including the twelve-hour preparations on holidays. Of these thousand hours a just allotment of so many hundred hours was to be made for Modern History, Ancient History, Political Theories, Greek Drama, Eighteenth-Century Prose, and Shakespeare. He then drew up a very complicated time-table, which would enable one to pay equal attention to all subjects. Balance in preparation was everything. What was the use of being able to score a hundred per cent. in Modern European History if Shakespeare was going to drag you in the mire?

Out of the daily six hours, three were to be devoted to the Optional Subjects and three to the Compulsory. In the morning the compulsory subjects, and Literature at night. European History needed all the freshness and sharpness of the morning brain, while it would be a real pleasure to read Literature in the evenings.

He put down for that day *Othello* and the Modern Period in Indian History. He would finish these two in about forty-eight hours and then take up Milton and Greek History.

And he settled down to this programme with a scowl on his face.

The Modern Period in Indian History, which he had to take up immediately, presented innumerable difficulties. The texts on the subject were many, the notes of class lectures very bulky. Moreover, if he went on studying the Modern Period, what was to happen to the Mediæval Period and the Ancient ? He could not afford to neglect those two important sections of Indian History. Could he now start at the beginning, with the arrival of the Aryans in India, and at a stretch go on to Lord Curzon's Viceroyalty ? That would mean, reckoning on Godstone's three volumes, the mastication of over a thousand pages. It was a noble ambition, no doubt, but hardly a sound one, because the university would not recognize your work and grant you a degree if you got a hundred per cent. in History and one per cent. in the other subjects? Chandran sat for nearly half an hour lost in this problem.

The household was up by this time. His father was in the garden, minutely examining the plants for evidence of any miracle that might have happened overnight. When he passed before Chandran's window he said, "You have got up very early to-day."

"I shall get up before five every day hereafter," said Chandran.

"Very good."

"This is November the first. My examinations are on the eighteenth of March. How many days is it from now?"

"About one hundred and thirty-eight——"

"About that," said Chandran. "It must be less because February, which comes before the examination month, has only twenty-eight days unless the leap year gives it a day more. So it must be less than one hundred and twenty-eight by three days. Do you know the total number of pages I have to read? Roughly about five thousand pages, four times over, not to speak of class lecture notes. About twenty thousand pages in one hundred and twenty days. That is the reason why I have to get up so early in the morning. I shall probably have to get up earlier still in course of time. I have drawn up a programme of work. Won't you step in and have a look at it ? "

Father came in and gazed at the sheet of paper on Chandran's table. He could not make anything of it. What he saw before him was a very intricate document, as complicated as a railway time-table. He honestly made an attempt to understand it and then said, " I don't follow this quite clearly." Chandran took the trouble to explain it to him. He also explained to him the problems that harassed him in studying History, and sought his advice. " I want to know if it would be safe to read only the Modern Period in Godstone and study the rest in notes." His father had studied science for his B.A. This consultation on an historical point puzzled him. He said, " I feel you ought not to take such risks."

Chandran felt disappointed. He had hoped that his father would agree with him in supplementing Godstone with the class notes. This advice irritated him. After all, Father had never been a history student.

" Father, you have no idea what splendid lectures

Ragavachar gives in the class. His lectures are the essence of all the books on the subject. If one reads his notes, one can pass even the I.C.S. examination."

"You know best," said Father. As he started back for the garden, he said, "Chandar, if you go to the market will you buy some wire-netting? Somebody is regularly stealing the jasmine from the creeper near the compound wall. I want to put up some kind of obstruction that side."

"That will spoil the appearance of the house, Father."

"But what are we to do? Somebody comes in even before dawn and steals the flowers."

"After all, only flowers," said Chandran, and Father went out muttering something.

Chandran returned to his work, having definitely made up his mind to study only the Modern Period in Godstone. He pulled out the book from the shelf, blew off the dust, and began at the Mogul Invasion. It was a heavy book with close print and shining pages, interspersed with smudgy pictures of kings dead and gone.

At nine he closed the book, having read five pages. He felt an immense satisfaction at having made a beginning.

While going in to breakfast he saw his younger

brother, Seenu, standing in the courtyard and looking at the crows on an areca-nut tree far off. He was just eight years old, and was studying in the Third Class in Albert Mission School. Chandran said to him, "Why do you waste the morning gazing at the sky?"

"I am waiting to bathe. Somebody is in the bathroom."

"It is only nine. What is the hurry for your bath? Do you want to spend the whole day before the bathroom? Go back to your desk. You will be called when the bathroom is vacant. Let me not catch you like this again!"

Seenu vanished from the spot. Chandran was indignant. In his days in the Albert Mission he had studied for at least two hours every morning. The boys in these days had absolutely no sense of responsibility.

His mother appeared from somewhere with the flower-basket in her hand. She was full of grievances: "Somebody takes away all the flowers in the garden. Is there no way of stopping this nuisance? Nobody seems to care for anything in this house." She was in a fault-finding mood. Not unusual at this hour. She had a variety of work to do in the mornings—tackling the milkman, the vegetable-seller, the oil-monger, and other tradespeople ; directing the work of the cook and of the servants ; gathering flowers for the daily worship ; and attending to all the eccentricities and wants of her husband and children.

Chandran knew that the worst one could do at that time was to argue with her. So he said soothingly, " We will lock the gate at night, and try to put up some wire-netting on the wall."

She replied, " Wire-netting ! It will make the house hideous ! Has your father been suggesting it again ? "

" No, no," Chandran said, " he just mentioned it as a last measure if nothing else is possible."

" I won't have it," Mother said decisively ; " something else has got to be done." Chandran said that steps should be taken, and asked himself what could be done short of digging a moat around the house and putting crocodiles in it. Mother, however, was appeased by this assurance. She explained mildly, " Your father spends nearly twenty-five rupees on the garden and nearly ten rupees on a gardener. What is the use of all this expense if we can't have a handful of flowers in the morning, for throwing on the gods in the *Puja* room ? "

§

That afternoon, while crossing the quadrangle, Chandran met Ragavachar, the Professor of History. He was about to pass him, paying the usual tribute of a meek salute, when Ragavachar called, " Chandran ! "

" Yes, sir," answered Chandran, much puzzled, having never been addressed by any professor outside the class. In a big college the professors could know personally only the most sycophantic or the most brilliant. Chandran was neither.

" What hour do you finish your work to-day ? "

" At four-thirty, sir."

" See me in my room at four-thirty."

" Yes, sir."

When told of this meeting Ramu asked, " Did you try to plant a bomb or anything in his house ? " Chandran retorted hotly that he didn't appreciate the joke. Ramu said that he was disappointed to hear this, and asked what Chandran wanted him to do. Chandran said, " Will you please shut up and try not to explain anything ? " They were sitting on the steps outside the lecture hall. Ramu got up and said, " If you want me, I shall be in the Union reading-room till five."

"We have *Othello* at three-thirty."

"I am not attending it," said Ramu, and was gone.

Chandran sat alone, worrying. Why had Ragavachar called him? He hadn't misbehaved; no library book overdue; there were one or two tests he hadn't attended, but Ragavachar never corrected any test paper. Or could it be that he had suddenly gone through all the test papers and found out that Chandran had not attended some of the tests? If it was only a reprimand, the professor would do it in the open class. Would any professor waive such an opportunity and do it in his room? For that matter, Ramu had not attended a single test in his life. Why was he not called? What did Ramu mean by going away in a temper? "Not attending it!" Seemed to be taking things easy.

The bell rang. Chandran rose and went in. He climbed the gallery steps and reached his seat. He opened the pages of *Othello*, placed a sheet of paper on the page, and took out his pen.

It was the Assistant Professor's subject. The Assistant Professor of English was Mr. Gajapathi, a frail man with a meagre moustache and heavy spectacles. He earned the hatred of the students by his teaching and of his colleagues by his conceit. He said everywhere that not ten persons in the world had understood Shakespeare ; he asserted that there were serious errors even in Fowler's *Modern English Usage* ; he corrected everybody's English ; he said that no Indian could ever write English ; this statement hurt all his colleagues, who prepared their lectures in English and wished to think that they wrote well. When he valued test or examination papers, he never gave anybody more than forty per cent. ; he constituted himself an authority on punctuation, and deducted half a mark per misplaced comma or semicolon in the papers that he corrected.

He entered the hall at a trot, jumped on the platform, opened his book, and began to read a scene in *Othello*. He read Shakespeare in a sing-song fashion, and with a vernacular twang. He stopped now and then to criticize other critics. Though Dowden had said so and so, Mr. Gajapathi was not prepared to be browbeaten by a big name. No doubt Bradley and others had done a certain amount of research in Shakespeare, but one couldn't accept all that they said as gospel truth. Gajapathi proved in endless instances how wrong others were.

Chandran attempted to take down notes, but they threatened to shape into something like the Sayings of Gajapathi. Chandran screwed the cap on his pen and sat back. Gajapathi never liked to see people sitting back and looking at him. He probably felt nervous when two hundred pairs of eyes stared at him. It was his habit to say, " Heads down and pencils busy, gentlemen," and " Listen to me with your pencils, gentlemen."

In due course he said, " Chandran, I see you taking a rest."

" Yes, sir."

" Don't say 'yes.' Keep your pen busy."

" Yes, sir." Chandran, with his head bent, began to scribble on the sheet of paper before him : " Oh, Gajapathi, Gajapathi ! When will you shut up ? Do you think that your lecture is very interesting and valuable ? In these two lines Shakespeare reveals the innermost core of Iago. *Gaja*, in Sanskrit, means elephant ; *pathy* is probably master. A fine name for you, you Elephant Master." And here followed the sketch of an elephant with spectacles on.

" Chandran, do I understand you are taking down notes ? "

" Yes, sir."

The bell rang. Gajapathi intended to continue the lecture even after the bell ; but two hundred copies of Verity's *Othello* shut with a loud report like the cracking of a rifle. The class was on its feet.

When he came down the gallery, Gajapathi said, "A moment, Chandran." Chandran stopped near the platform as the others streamed past him. Everybody seemed to want him to-day.

Gajapathi said, "I should like to see your lecture notes."

Chandran was nonplussed for a moment. If he remembered aright he had scribbled an elephant. The other things he did not clearly recollect; but he knew that they were not meant for Gajapathi's scrutiny. He wondered for a moment whether he should escape with a lie, but felt that Gajapathi did not deserve that honour. He said, "Honestly, I have not taken down anything, sir. If you will excuse me, I must go now. I have to see Professor Ragavachar."

As he came near the Professor's room, Chandran felt very nervous. He adjusted his coat and buttoned it up. He hesitated for a moment before the door. He suddenly pulled himself up. Why this cowardice? Why should he be afraid of Ragavachar or anybody? Human being to human being. Remove those spectacles, the turban, and the long coat, and let Ragavachar appear only in a loin-cloth, and Mr. Ragavachar would lose three-quarters of his appearance. Where was the sense in feeling nervous before a pair of spectacles, a turban, and a black long coat ?

" Good-evening, sir," said Chandran, stepping in.

Ragavachar looked up from a bulky red book that he was reading. He took time to switch his mind off his studies and comprehend the present.

" Well ? " he said, looking at Chandran.

" You asked me to see you at four-thirty, sir."

" Yes, yes. Sit down."

Chandran lowered himself to the edge of a chair. Ragavachar leaned back and spent some time looking at the ceiling. Chandran felt a slight thirsty sensation, but he recollected his vision of Ragavachar in a loin-cloth, and regained his self-confidence.

" My purpose in calling you now is to ascertain your views on the question of starting an Historical Association in the college."

Saved ! Chandran sat revelling in the sense of relief he now felt.

" What do you think of it ? "

" I think it is a good plan, sir," and he wondered why he was chosen for this consultation.

" What I want you to do," went on the commanding voice, " is to arrange for an inaugural meeting on the fifteenth instant. We shall decide the programme afterwards."

" Very well, sir," said Chandran.

" You will be the Secretary of the Association. I shall be its President. The meeting must be held on the fifteenth."

" Don't you think, sir . . ." Chandran began.

" What don't I think ? " asked the Professor.

" Nothing, sir."

" I hate these sneaky half-syllables," the Professor said. " You were about to say something. I won't proceed till I know what you were saying."

Chandran cleared his throat and said, " Nothing, sir. I was only going to say that some one else might do better as a secretary."

" I suppose you can leave that to my judgment."

" Yes, sir."

" I hope you don't question the need for starting the association."

" Certainly not, sir."

" Very good. I for one feel that the amount of ignorance on historical matters is appalling. The only way in which we can combat it is to start an association and hold meetings and read papers."

" I quite understand, sir."

" Yet you ask me why we should have this association ! "

"No, I did not doubt it."

"H'm. You talk the matter over with one or two of your friends, and see me again with some definite programme for the Inaugural Meeting."

Chandran rose.

"You seem to be in a hurry to go," growled the tiger.

"No, sir," said Chandran, and sat down again.

"If you are in a hurry to go, I can't stop you because it is past four-thirty, and you are free to leave the college premises. On the other hand, if you are not in a hurry, I have some more details to discuss with you."

"Yes, sir."

"There is no use repeating 'Yes, sir; yes, sir.' You don't come forward with any constructive suggestion."

"I will talk it over with some friends and come later, sir."

"Good-evening. You may go now."

§

Chandran emerged from the Professor's room with his head bowed in thought. He felt a slight distaste for himself as a secretary. He felt that he was on the verge of losing his personality. Now he would have to be like Natesan, the Union Secretary. One's head would be full of nothing but meetings to be arranged ! He was now condemned to go about with a fixed idea, namely, the Inaugural Meeting. The Inaugural Meeting by itself was probably not a bad thing, if it were also the final meeting ; but they would expect him to arrange at least half a dozen meetings before March : readings of papers on mock subjects, heavy lectures by paunchy hags, secretary's votes of thanks, and endless other things. He hated the whole business. He would have to sit through the lectures, wait till the lights were put out and the doors locked, and go out into the night with a headache, foregoing the walk by the river with Ramu. Ah, Ramu ; that fellow behaved rather queerly in the afternoon, going off in a temper like that.

Chandran went to the reading-room in the Union. None of the half a dozen heads bent over the illustrated journals belonged to Ramu. Chandran had a hope that Ramu might be in the chess-room. He was not the sort to play chess, but he occasionally might be found in the company that stood around and watched a game of chess, shutting out light and air from the players. But to-day the game of chess seemed to be going on without Ramu's supervision; nor was he to be found in the ping-pong room. Chandran descended the Union steps in thorough discontent.

He turned his steps to the river, which was a stone's throw from the college. He walked along the sand. The usual crowd was there—girls with jasmine in their hair, children at play, students loafing about, and elderly persons at their constitutionals. Chandran enjoyed immensely an evening on the river bank: he stared at the girls, pretended to be interested in the children, guffawed at friends, perambulated about twice or thrice, and then walked to the lonely Nallappa's Grove and smoked a cigarette there. Ramu's company and his running commentary lent vitality to the whole experience.

But to-day his mind was clogged, and Ramu was absent. Chandran was beginning to feel bored. He started homeward.

It was a little past seven when he turned into the Second Cross road in Lawley Extension. He stood before Ramu's gate and shouted, "Ramu!" Ramu came out.

"Why were you not in the reading-room?"

"I waited, and thought that you would be late and came away."

"You were not by the river."

"I returned home and went for a walk along the Trunk Road."

"What did you mean by going away like that to the reading-room, so abruptly?"

"I wanted to read the magazines."

"I don't believe it. You went away in a temper. I wonder why you are so lacking in patience!"

"What about your temper? You meet Ragavachar and are worried, and a fellow says something lightly and you flare up!"

Chandran ignored the charge. He seized upon the subject of Ragavachar. He gave a full account of the amazing interview. They stood on the road, talking the matter over and over again, for nearly two hours.

When Chandran went home his father said, "Nine o'clock." Later, when he was about to go to bed, Father asked, "Your plan of study not come into force yet?" That question hurt Chandran's conscience. He went to his table and stood looking at the programme he had sketched out in the morning. Not much of it was clear now. He went to bed and his conscience gnawed at him in the dark till about eleven. He had spent the morning in drawing plans and the rest of the day somehow. First of

November gone, irrevocably gone, and wasted; six of the forty-eight hours for *Othello* and Godstone thrown on the scrap-heap.

§

The Inaugural Meeting troubled Chandran day and night, and he was unable to make any progress in *Othello* and Godstone. His notions as to what one did on the day of the meeting were very vague. He faintly thought that at such a meeting people sat around, drank tea, shook hands with each other, and felt inaugural.

Five mornings before the meeting, in a fit of desperation, he flung aside his Godstone, and started for Natesan's room. If ever there was a man to guide another in these matters, it was Natesan. He had been twice the Secretary of the Sanskrit Association, once its Vice-President, Secretary of the Philosophy Association, of a Social Service League, and now of the Union. Heaven knew what other things he was going to be. He must have conducted nearly a hundred meetings in his college life. Though Chandran had sometimes dreaded meeting this man, now he felt happy when he knocked on his door and found him in. It was a very narrow room with a small window opening on the twisting Kabir Street, and half-filled with a sleeping cot, and the remaining space given over to the four legs of a very big table, on which books were heaped. One opened the door and stepped on the cot. Natesan was reclining on a roll of bedding and studying. He was very pleased to see Chandran, and invited him to take a seat on the cot.

Chandran poured out his troubles. "What does one do on the inaugural day?"

"A lengthy address is delivered, and then the chairman thanks the lecturer, and the secretary thanks the lecturer and the chairman, and the audience rise to go home."

"No tea or anything?"

"Oh, no. Nothing of the sort. Who is to pay for the tea?"

And then hearing of Chandran's vagueness and difficulties, Natesan suggested the Principal for the address, and Professor Ragavachar for the chair. After his interview with Natesan, Chandran realized that a secretary's life was a tormented one. He was now in a position to appreciate the services of not only Natesan, but also of Alam, the Secretary of the Literary Association, of Rajan, the Philosophy Association Secretary, of Moorty, the Secretary of the Economics Association, the people who were responsible for all the meetings in the college. Chandran realized that there was more in these meetings than met the eye or entered the ear. Each meeting was a supreme example of human endeavour, of selfless service. For what did a secretary after all gain by sweating? No special honours from the authorities nor extra marks in the examinations. Far from it. More often ridicule from classmates and frowns from professors, if something went wrong. The bothers of a secretary were: a clash with other secretaries over the date of a meeting; finding a speaker; finding a subject for the speaker; and getting an audience for the subject.

That day Chandran skipped nearly two periods in order to see the Principal. The peon squatting before the Principal's room would not let him in. Chandran pleaded and begged. The peon spoke in whispers, and commanded Chandran to talk in whispers. Chandran whispered that he had to see the Principal, whispered a threat, whispered an admonition, in whispers cringed and begged, but the peon was adamant.

"I have orders not to let anybody in," said the peon. He was an old man, grown grey in college service, that is in squatting before the Principal's office door. His name was Aziz.

"Look here, Aziz," Chandran said in a soothing tone, "why can't anybody see him now?"

"It is not for me to ask. I won't let anybody in. He is very busy."

"Busy with what?"

"What do you care?" Aziz asked haughtily.

"Is he given his thousand a month to sit behind that door and refuse to see people?"

At this the servant lost his temper, and asked, "Who are you to question it?" Chandran gave some stinging answer to this. It was a great strain to carry on the conversation, the whole thing having to be conducted in whispers. Chandran realized that it was no use losing one's temper. He tried strategy now. He said, "Aziz, I have an old coat at home; not a tear in it. Will you come for it to-morrow morning?"

"What time?"

"Any time you please. I live in Lawley Extension."

"Yes, I know. I will find out your house."

"Give me a slip of paper."

Aziz tore out a slip from a bundle hung on the door. Chandran wrote his name on it and sent it in.

Aziz came out of the room in a few minutes and said that Chandran might go in. Chandran adjusted his coat and entered.

" Good-morning, sir."

" Good-morning."

Chandran delivered a short preamble on the Historical Association, and stated his request. The Principal took out a small black diary, turned over its pages, and said, " The fifteenth evening is free. All right."

" Thank you, sir," said Chandran, and remained standing for a few minutes. He himself could not say what he was waiting there for. His business had been completed too rapidly. He didn't know whether he ought to say something more or leave the room abruptly. The Principal took out a cigarette and lighted it. " Well ? "

" We are . . . We are very grateful to you, sir, for your great kindness."

" Oh, it's all right. Don't mention it."

" May I take my leave ? "

" Yes."

" Thank you, sir. Good-morning." Chandran marched out of the room. When he passed Aziz he said, " What a bad fellow you are, you wouldn't let me in ! "

"Master, I do my duty and get a bad name. What am I to do? Can I see you to-morrow morning?"

"I shall ask the peon at our gate not to let you in."

"Oh, master, I am a poor old fellow, always shivering with cold. Don't disappoint me. If you give me a coat, I shall always remember you as my saviour."

"All right. Come to-morrow," whispered Chandran, and passed on.

He went to Ragavachar's room and announced that the Principal had consented to deliver the inaugural address. Ragavachar did not appear excited by the news. He growled, after some rumination, "I am not sure if his address will be suitable for an Historical Association."

"I think, sir, he can adjust himself."

"One hopes so."

"You must take the chair, sir."

"I suppose . . . H'm." Nothing further was said. Having moved with him closely for ten days Chandran understood it to mean consent.

"May I go, sir?"

"Yes."

CHAPTER THREE

THE fifteenth of November was a busy day for Chandran. He spent a great part of the morning in making arrangements for the meeting in the evening.

Two days before, he had issued printed notices over his signature to all the members of the staff, and to all the important lawyers, doctors, officials, and teachers in the town. From every board in the college his notices invited every one to be present at the meeting.

As a result of this, on the fifteenth at five in the evening, while Chandran was still arranging the dais and the chairs in the lecture hall of the college, the audience began to arrive.

The college peon, Aziz, lent him a stout hand in making the arrangements. The old coat had done the trick. Aziz personally attended to the arrangement of the chairs in the front row. He arranged the chairs and the table on the dais. He gave a gorgeous setting to the Historical Association. He spread a red cloth on the dais, and a green baize on the table. He illuminated the hall with petrol lamps.

As the guests arrived, Chandran ran to the veranda and received them and conducted them to their seats. At 5.15 almost all the chairs were occupied ; all the seats in the gallery were also filled. Students of the college who came late hung on to the banisters.

The Principal and Professor Ragavachar arrived and stopped in the veranda. Chandran flitted about uncertainly, and invited them in. The Principal looked at his watch and said, " Five minutes more. We shall stay here till five-thirty."

Ragavachar adjusted his spectacles and murmured, " Yes, yes."

Some more guests arrived. Chandran showed them their seats. Ramu was all the time at his side, running errands, helping him, asking questions, and not always receiving an answer.

" What a crowd ! " Ramu said.

"You see . . ." began Chandran, and saw the Headmaster of the Albert Mission School arriving and ran forward to meet him. Chandran returned after seating the Headmaster in the hall.

Ramu said, "It looks as if you were giving a dinner-party to the town folk."

Chandran said, his eyes scanning the drive for visitors, " Yes, it looks like that. Only flowers, scents, and a dinner missing to complete the picture."

Ramu asked, " Shall I wait for you at the end of the lecture ? " and was not destined to receive an answer. For, at this moment, Ragavachar looked at his watch and said, " It is five-thirty, shall we begin ? "

" Yes, sir."

The Secretary led the speaker and the Chairman to their chairs on the dais, and occupied a third chair placed on the edge of the dais.

After the cheering and stamping had subsided, Ragavachar rose, put on his spectacles, and began, " Ladies and gentlemen, I am not going to presume to introduce to you the lecturer of this evening. I do not propose to stand between you and the lecturer. I shall take only a few minutes, perhaps only a few seconds, to enlighten you on a few facts concerning our association. . . ." He then filled the hall with his voice for a full forty minutes. The audience gathered from his speech that an Historical Association represented his faith in life ; it was a vision which guided him in all his activities. The audience also understood that darkness prevailed in the minds of over ninety per cent. of human beings, and that he expected the association to serve the noble end of dispelling this darkness. Great controversial fires were raging over very vital matters in Indian History. And what did they find around them ? The public went about their business as if nothing was happening. How could one expect these fires to be extinguished if the great public did not show an intelligent appreciation of the situation and lend a helping hand ? To quote an instance : everybody learnt in the secondary school history book that Sirajudowlla locked some of the East Indian Company people in a very small room, and allowed them to die of suffocation. This was the well-known Black Hole of Calcutta. There were super-historians who appeared at a later stage in one's education and said that there had been neither Black nor Hole nor Calcutta. He was not going to indicate his own views on the question. But he only wished to convey to the minds of the audience, to the public at large, to all intelligent humanity in general, what a state of bloody feud existed in the realm of Indian History. True history was neither fiction nor philosophy. It was a hardy science. And to place Indian History there, an Assocation was indispensable. If he were asked what the country needed most urgently, he would not say Self-Government or Economic Independence, but a clarified, purified Indian History.

After this he repeated that he would not stand between the lecturer and his audience, and, calling upon Professor Brown to deliver the Inaugural Address, sat down.

As Professor Brown got up there was great applause. He looked about, put his right hand in his trouser pocket, held his temples with his left hand, and began. He looked at Chandran and said that he had not bargained for this, a meeting of this dimension and importance, when he acceded to the Secretary's request. Chandran tapped the arms of his chair with his fingers, looked down and smiled, almost feeling that he had played a deep game on the Principal. The lecturer said that he had consented to deliver an address this evening, thinking that he was to be at the opening of a very simple Association. From what Ragavachar said, he understood it to be something that was of national importance. If he had known this, his place now would be in one of the chairs that he saw before him, and he would have left the responsible task to better persons. However, it was too late to do anything now. He hoped that he would have an occasion to settle his score with Chandran.

The audience enjoyed every word of this. People who had awaited Brown's humour were fully satisfied.

Professor Brown traced his relations with History from the earliest times when he was in a private school in Somerset to the day on which he entered Oxford, where he shook History off his person, because he found the subject as treacherous as a bog at night. Thereafter, for his degree, he studied Literature, and regularly spent some hours of private study on History. "I can now give a fairly coherent account of mankind's 'doings,' if I may borrow an expression from the composition books that I correct. But don't ask me the date of anything. In all History I remember only 1066."

He held the audience for about an hour thus, with nothing very serious, nothing profound, but with the revelation of a personality, with delicious reminiscences, touched with humour and occasional irony.

He sat down after throwing at his audience this advice: "Like Art, History must be studied for its own sake; and so, if you are to have an abiding interest in it, take it up after you leave the university. For outside the university you may read your history in any order; from the middle work back to the beginning of things or in any way you like, and nobody will measure how many facts you have rammed into your poor head. Facts are, after all, a secondary matter in real History."

Ragavachar inwardly fretted and fumed at the speech. If the lecturer had been any one else than Brown, the Principal of the college, he would have taken the speech to bits and thrown it to the four winds, and pulled out the tongue of the lecturer and cut it off. At the end of the lecture, he merely rose and thanked the lecturer on behalf of the audience and sat down. When Chandran rose to propose a hearty vote of thanks to the lecturer and to the chairman for their great kindness in consenting to conduct the meeting, it acted as a signal for the audience to rise and go home. A babble broke out. Chandran's voice could hardly be heard except by a select few in the very first row.

CHAPTER FOUR

CHANDRAN put off everything till the Inaugural Meeting was over. He consoled himself with the fact that he had wasted several months so far, and a fortnight more, added to that account, should not matter. He had resolved that the moment the meeting was over he would get up at 4.30 instead of 5 a.m. as decided originally. The time wasted in a fortnight could then be made up by half an hour's earlier rising every day. He would also return home at seven in the evening instead of at seven-thirty. This would give him a clear gain of an hour a day over his previous programme. He hoped to make up the ninety study hours, at six hours a day, lost between the first of November and the fifteenth, in the course of ninety days.

This was a sop to his clamouring conscience. He thought now he would be able to get up at four-thirty on the following morning and begin his whirlwind programme of study. But man can only propose. He was destined to throw away two more mornings. On the night of the big meeting, before going to bed, he spent some time on the carpet in the hall, gossiping with his mother. He announced that he would get up at four-thirty next morning.

Father, who appeared to be reading a newspaper in the veranda, exclaimed, " So after all ! " This remark disturbed Chandran. But he remained silent, hoping that it would discourage his father from uttering further remarks. Father, however, was not to be kept off so easily. The newspaper rustled on the veranda, and five minutes later came the remark, "Since this is the third time you have made a resolution, it is likely you will stick to it, because every plan must have two trials." Chandran rose and went on to the veranda. His father was in a puckish, teasing mood. As soon as Chandran came out, he looked at him over his spectacles and asked, " Don't you agree with me ? "

" What, Father ? "

" That a plan must have two trials."

Chandran felt uncomfortable. " You see, Father, but for this dreadful meeting I should have done ninety hours of study, according to my time-table. I shall still make it up. I shall not be available to any one from to-morrow." He gave a glowing account of what he was going to do from the next morning onwards.

Father said that he was quite pleased to hear it. He said, " If you get up at four-thirty, do wake me up also. I want to wait and catch the scoundrel who steals the flowers in the morning."

Mother's voice came from the hall, " So, after all, you are doing something ! "

" Hardly my fault that," Father shouted back. " I offered to put up wire-fencing over the wall."

" Why, do you want to give the thief some wire in addition to the flowers ? "

Father was greatly affected by this taunt.

Mother added fuel to it by remarking, " Twenty-five rupees on the garden and not a single petal of any flower for the gods in the *Puja* room."

Father was very indignant. He behaved like a mediæval warrior goaded by his lady-love into slaying a dragon. Father dropped a hint that the flower thief would be placed at her feet next day, alive or dead.

Next morning Chandran was awakened by his alarum clock. He went to his father's room and woke him up. After that he went to the bathroom for a cold bath.

In ten minutes Chandran was at his table. He adjusted the light, drew the chair into position, and pondered over the piece of paper on which he had written a time-table.

His father entered the room, carrying a stout bamboo staff in his hand. Behind him came Seenu, armed with another stick. There was the light of a hunter in Father's eyes, and Seenu was bubbling over with enthusiasm. Chandran was slightly annoyed at this intrusion. But Father whispered an apology, and requested, " Put out that light. If it is seen in your room, the thief will not come near the house."

" So much the better. Mother can take the flowers in the morning," said Chandran.

" He will come some other day."

" From now on, at least till March, there is no fear of this room ever being without a light at this hour. So the flower thief will be away till March. Let us catch him after that."

" Oh, that is all far-fetched. I must get him to-day. It doesn't matter if you lose about an hour. You can make it up later."

Chandran blew out the lamp and sat in the dark. Father and Seenu went out into the garden. Chandran sat in his chair for some time. He rose and stood looking out of the window. It was very dark in the garden.

Chandran began to wonder what his father and brother were doing, and how far they had progressed with the thief. His curiosity increased. He went into the garden, and moved cautiously along the shadows, and heard hoarse whispers coming from behind a big sprawling croton.

" Oh, it is Chandran," said a voice.

Father and Seenu were crouching behind the croton.

" Don't make any noise," Father whispered to Chandran.

Chandran found the tactics weak. He took command. It seemed to him waste to concentrate all the forces in one place. He ordered his father to go a little forward and conceal himself behind a rose bush ; and his younger brother to prowl around the backyard, while he himself would be here and there and everywhere, moving with panther-like steps from cover to cover.

There was a slight hitch in the campaign. Seenu objected to the post he was allotted. It was still dark, and the backyard had a mysterious air. Chandran called him a coward and several other things, and asked him why he had left his bed at all if he could not be of some use to people.

In about an hour the sun came out and revealed the jasmine and other plants bare of flowers. Father merely looked at them and said, "We must get up at four o'clock, not at four-thirty."

Next day Chandran was out of bed at four, and with his father hunting in the garden. Nothing happened for about ten minutes. Then a slight noise was heard near the gate. Father was behind the rose bush, and Chandran had pressed himself close to the compound wall. A figure heaved itself on to the portion of the wall next to the gate, and jumped into the garden. The stranger looked about for a fraction of a second and went towards the jasmine creeper in a business-like way.

Hardly had he plucked half a dozen flowers when father and son threw themselves on him with war-cries. It was quite a surprise for Chandran to see his father so violent. They dragged the thief into the house, held him down, and shouted to mother to wake up and light the lamp.

The light showed the thief to be a middle-aged man, bare bodied, with matted hair, wearing only a loin-cloth. The loin-cloth was ochre-coloured, indicating that he was a *sanyasi*, an ascetic. Father relaxed his hold on noticing this.

Mother screamed, "Oh, hold him, hold him."

She was shaking with excitement. "Take him away and give him to the police."

Chandran said to the thief, "You wear the garb of a *sanyasi*, and yet you do this sort of thing!"

"Is he a *sanyasi*?" Mother asked, and noticed the colour of the thief's loin-cloth. "Ah, leave him alone, let him go." She was seized with fear now. The curse of a holy man might fall on the family. "You can go, sir," she said respectfully.

Chandran was cynical. "What, Mother, you are frightened of every long hair and ochre dress you see. If you are really a holy man, why should you do this?"

"What have I done?" asked the thief.

"Jumping in and stealing flowers."

"If you lock the gate, how else can I get in than by jumping over the wall? As for stealing flowers, flowers are there, God-given. What matters it whether you throw the flowers on the gods, or I do it. It is all the same."

"But you should ask our permission."

"You are all asleep at that hour, and I don't wish to disturb you. I can't wait until you get up because my worship is over before sunrise."

Mother interposed and said, "You can go now, sir. If you want flowers you can take them. There couldn't be a better way of worship than giving flowers to those who really worship."

"Truly said, Mother," said the holy man. "I should certainly have asked your permission but for the fact that none of you are awake at that hour."

"I shall be awake," said Chandran, "from to-morrow."

"Do you use these flowers for your worship, Mother?" asked the stranger.

"Certainly, every day. I never let a day go without worship."

"Ah, I did not know that. I had thought that here, as in many other bungalows, flowers were kept only for ornament. I am happy to hear that they are put to holy use. Hereafter I shall take only a handful and leave the rest for your worship. May I take leave of you now?" He crossed the hall and descended the veranda steps.

Father said to Chandran, "Take the gate key and open the gate. How can he get out?"

"If you leave him alone, he will jump over the wall and go," mumbled Chandran sourly as he took the gate key from the nail on the veranda wall.

CHAPTER FIVE

§

NOVEMBER to March was a very busy period for Chandran. He got up every day at four-thirty in the morning, and did not get to bed until eleven. He practised his iron scheme of study to the letter. By the beginning of March he was well up in every subject. There were still a few inevitable dark corners in his mind : a few hopeless controversies among Shakespearian Scholars, a few impossible periods in History like the muddle that was called the mediæval South Indian History, early Christianity with warring popes and kings, and feudalism. He allowed the muddle to remain undisturbed in his mind ; he got into the habit of postponing the mighty task of clarifying these issues to a distant favourable day. He usually encouraged himself in all this vagueness by saying that even if he lost thirty marks in each paper owing to these doubts he would still be well within the reach of seventy in each, and, out of this, allowing twenty for defective presentation and examiners' eccentricities, he would still get fifty marks in each paper, which would be ten more than was necessary for a pass degree.

He had a few other achievements to his credit. Before March he conducted about eight meetings of the Historical Association. He himself read a paper on "The Lesser-known Aspects of Mauryan Polity."

The Historical Association was responsible for two interesting contacts. He came to know Veeraswami, the revolutionary, and Mohan, the poet.

Veeraswami was a dark, stocky person, about twenty-two years old. One day he came to Chandran and offered to read a paper on "The Aids to British Expansion in India." Chandran was delighted. He had never met any one who volunteered to address the Association. On a fateful day, to an audience of thirty-five, Veeraswami read his paper. It was the most violent paper ever read before an association. It pilloried Great Britain before the Association, and ended by hoping that the British would be ousted from India by force. Ragavachar, who was present at the meeting, felt very uncomfortable. Next day he received a note from

Brown, the custodian of British prestige, suggesting that in future papers meant to be read before the Association should be first sent to him. This infuriated Chandran so much that he thought of resigning till Ragavachar assured him that he would not get his degree if he tried these antics. Chandran sought Veeraswami and told him of the turmoil that his paper had caused, and consulted him on the ways and means to put an end to Brown's autocracy. Veeraswami suggested that he should be allowed to read a paper on "The Subtleties of Imperialism," without sending the paper to Brown for his approval. Chandran declined this offer, explaining that he did not wish to be expelled from the college. Veeraswami asked why not, and called Chandran a coward. Chandran had a feeling that he had got into bed with a porcupine. Veeraswami bristled with prejudices and violence. Imperialism was his favourite demon. He believed in smuggling arms into the country, and, on a given day, shooting all the Englishmen. He assured Chandran that he was even then preparing for that great work. His education, sleep, contacts, and everything, were a preparation. He was even then gathering followers. He seemed to have considered this plan in all its aspects. Indians were hopelessly underfed and sickly. He proposed to cure hunger by encouraging the use of coconuts and the fruits of cactus for food. He was shortly going to issue pamphlets in Tamil, Telugu, and English on the subject. In regard to sickness he believed that the British encouraged it in order to provide a permanent market for the British drug manufacturers. He was going to defeat that plan by propagating the nature-cure idea. After thus improving the physique of the masses he would take charge of their minds. He would assume the garb of a village worker, a rural reconstruction maniac, but secretly prepare the mind of the peasantry for revolution.

After that Veeraswami never gave Chandran a moment's peace. In all leisure hours Chandran lived in terror of being caught by Veeraswami, which invariably happened. If Chandran went to the reading-room, Veeraswami was sure to hunt him down; if he went into the ping-pong room, he would be chased even there. So Chandran took to slinking out and going to a secluded spot on the river bank. This almost led to a misunderstanding with Ramu, who thought that Chandran was avoiding him. In the evenings, too, Veeraswami would catch Chandran and follow him everywhere. Veeraswami would talk all the evening as Ramu and Chandran followed him with the look of a sacrificial goat in their eyes.

The other person whom the Historical Association brought in, Mohan, was less troublesome. He sidled up to Chandran one afternoon as the latter sat over his coffee in the Union Restaurant, and asked if a meeting could be arranged where some poems might be read. Chandran felt quite thrilled to meet a poet in the flesh. He never read poetry for pleasure, but he had a great admiration for poets. Chandran asked the other to take a seat and offered him a cup of coffee.

" Have your poems anything to do with History ? "

" I don't understand you."

" I want to know if they deal with historical facts. Something like a poem on the Mogul Emperors and things of that type. Otherwise it would not be easy to get them read before the Historical Association."

" I am sorry you are so narrow-minded. You want everything to stay in water-tight compartments. When will you get a synthetic view of things ? Why should you think that poetry is different from history ? "

Chandran felt that he was being dragged into dangerous zones. He said, " Please let me know what your subjects are."

"Why should a poem have any subject? Is it not enough that there it is in itself?"

Chandran was thoroughly mystified. He asked, "You write in English or in Tamil?"

"Of course in English. It is the language of the world."

"Why don't you read your poems before the Literary Association?"

"Ah, do you think any such thing is possible with grandmother Brown as its president? As long as he is in this college no original work will ever be possible. He is very jealous, won't tolerate a pinch of original work. Go and read before the Literary Association, for the two-hundredth time, a rehash of his lecture notes on Wordsworth or Eighteenth Century Prose, and he will permit it. He won't stand anything else."

"I should certainly like to read your poems myself, but I don't see how it will be possible before the Association."

"If you have properly understood History as a record of human culture and development, you can't fail to see poetry as an integral part of it. If poems are to be read anywhere, it must be before an Historical Association."

When Chandran asked for permission to arrange

this meeting, Ragavachar ruled it out. He said that he did not care to have all sorts of versifiers come and contaminate the Association with their stuff. As he conveyed the refusal to Mohan, Chandran felt a great pity for the poet. He liked the poet. He was fascinated by his obscure statements. He desired to cultivate his friendship. He expressed his willingness to have some of the poems read to him. The only time he could spare was the evening, after the college was over. So the next evening he cancelled his walk and listened to verse. Ramu told Chandran not to expect him to sit down and enjoy that kind of entertainment, and went away before Mohan arrived.

Chandran hated his room in the evenings, but now he resigned himself to suffer in the cause of poetry.

Mohan came, with a bundle of typed sheets under his arm. After giving him a seat, Chandran asked, "How many poems have you brought?"

"A selection of about twenty-five, that is all."

"I hope we can finish them before seven," said Chandran, "because at seven-thirty I have to sit down to my studies."

"Oh, yes," said the poet, and began. He read far into the evening. The poems were on a wide variety of subjects—from a Roadside Grass-seller to the Planet in Its Orbit ; from Lines suggested by an Ant to the Dying Musician. All conceivable things seemed to have incited Mohan to anger, gloom, despair, and defiance. Some had rhymes, some had not ; some had a beginning, some had no end, some had no middle. But most of the poems mystified Chandran. After a time he gave up all attempt to understand them. He sat passively, listening, as the poet read by the twilight. He sighed with relief when the poet put down the twenty-fifth poem. The clock showed seven-fifteen. Chandran suggested a short stroll.

Chandran had a slight headache. The poet was hoarse with reading. During the stroll Chandran suggested, " Why don't you try to get some of the poems published in a paper ? "

" By every post I receive my poems back," said the poet. " For the last five years I have been trying to get my poems accepted. I have tried almost all the papers and magazines in the world—England, America, Canada, South Africa, Australia, and our own country. I must have spent a fortune in postage."

Chandran expressed his admiration for the other for still writing so much.

"I can no more help writing than I can help breathing," said the poet. "I shall go on writing till my fingers are paralysed. Every day I write. I hardly read any of the class texts. I know I shall fail. I don't care. I hope some day I shall come across an editor or publisher who is not stupid."

"Oh, you will very soon be a famous man," said Chandran with conviction.

§

In March Chandran lost about six pounds in weight. He hardly thought of anything, saw anybody, or did anything, except study. The college now existed only for the classroom, and the classroom only for the lectures. Everybody in the college was very serious and purposeful. Even Gajapathi now devoted less of his time to attacks on critics than to lectures that would be useful in the examination.

On the last day of the term there was an air of conclusion about everything. Every professor and lecturer came to the end of his subject and closed his book. Brown shut Sophocles and ended the year with the hope that his pupils' interest in literature would long survive the examination. He left the class amid great cheering and clapping of hands. Gajapathi put away his copy of *Othello*, and hoped that he had presented Shakespeare's mind clearly to his class ; he also hoped that after the examination they would all be in a position to form independent judgments of their own. The Professor of European History closed the year with the League of Nations. The last period on the last day was Indian History. Ragavachar growled out the full stop with a summary of the Montague-Chelmsford Reforms, and left the class after warning them not to disturb the other classes by cheering and clapping.

They had their Class Socials that evening. A group photo, with the Principal sitting in the centre, was taken. A large lunch was eaten, and coffee drunk. Songs were sung, speeches were made, everybody wished everybody else success in the examination ; professors shook hands with the students, and students shook hands with each other. Everybody was soft and sentimental. They did everything short of shedding tears at the parting.

As they dispersed and went home, Chandran was aware that he had passed the very last moment in his college life, which had filled the major portion of his waking hours for the last four years. There would be no more college for him from to-morrow. He would return to it a fortnight hence for the examination and (hoping for the best) pass it, and pass out into the world, forever out of Albert College. He felt very tender and depressed.

PART TWO

CHAPTER SIX

WITHIN six months of becoming a graduate Chandran began to receive suggestions from relatives and elderly friends of the family as to what he should do with himself. Till this time it had never occurred to him that he ought to be doing anything at all. But now, wherever he went, he was pestered with the question, "Now what do you propose to do?"

"I have not thought of anything yet."

"Why don't you go to Madras and study Law?"

There was his uncle in Nellore who wrote to him that he ought to do something and try to settle in life. There was his mother's cousin who advised him to study Law. There was his Madras uncle who said that staying in Malgudi would not lead him anywhere, but that he ought to go to a big city and see people. He had immense faith in seeing people. He himself volunteered to give a letter of introduction to some big man, an auditor in the railways, who could in his turn give a further introduction to some one else, and finally fix up Chandran in the railways. This uncle seemed to live in an endless dream of introductory letters. Several relatives, chiefly women, asked him why he did not sit for the Indian Civil Service or the Indian Audit Service examination. Chandran felt flattered by their faith in him. There were others who said that there was nothing like a business occupation; start on a small capital and open a shop; independence and profit. All sorts of persons advised him to apply for a clerk's post in some Government office. Nothing like Government service, they said; on the first of the month you were sure of your money; security. Chandran had a feeling of persecution. He opened his heart to his father when the latter was trimming the roses early one morning.

"I am sorry, Father, that I ever passed the B.A."

"Why?"

"Why should everybody talk about my career? Why can't they mind their business?"

"It is the way of the world. You must not let that upset you. It is just a form of courtesy, you see."

Then they began to talk of Chandran's future. His father gathered that Chandran had a vague desire to go to England and do something there. He did not consider the plan absurd himself.

"What do you propose to do in England?"

"I want to get a doctorate or something and come back, and then some quiet lectureship in some college will suit me wonderfully. Plenty of independence and leisure."

After that Chandran went about with a freer mind. To his persecutors he would say, "I am going to England next year." Some demanded why he was not starting immediately. Chandran told them, "We can't go to England on an impulse, can we?"

And now, without college or studies to fetter him, Chandran was enjoying a freedom he had never experienced in his life before. From his infant class up to B.A., a period of over sixteen years, he had known nothing like this holiday, which stretched over six months. He would have enjoyed this freedom still more if Ramu had been there with him. After the results were announced Ramu disappeared. He went away to Bombay in search of employment, and drifted all over Northern India without securing any. Chandran received only one card informing him that Ramu had joined the law course in Poona.

So Chandran was compelled to organize his

life without Ramu. He became a member of the Town Public Library, and read an enormous quantity of fiction and general literature. He discovered Carlyle. He found that after all Shakespeare had written some stirring dramas, and that several poets were not as dull as they were made out to be. There was no scheme or order in his study. He read books just as they came. He read a light humorist and switched on to Carlyle, and from there pounced on Shakespeare, and then wandered to Shaw and Wells. The thing that mattered most to him was that the book should be enjoyable, and he ruthlessly shut books that threatened to bore him.

After spending a large part of the day with books he went out in the evening for long walks, necessarily alone, since most of his friends had gone away. He went on long rambles by the river, returned home late, and sat up for an hour or two chatting with his parents, and then read a little in bed. As he settled down to this routine he got used to it and enjoyed this quiet life. Every day as he went through one item he eagerly looked forward to the next, and then the next, till he looked forward to the delicious surge of sleep as he put away his book for the night.

CHAPTER SEVEN

§

IT was on one of his river ramblings that he met Malathi and thought that he would not have room for anything else in his mind. No one can explain the attraction between two human beings. It happens.

One evening he came to the river, and was loafing along it, when he saw a girl, about fifteen years old, playing with her younger sister on the sands. Chandran had been in the habit of staring at every girl who sat on the sand, but he had never felt before the acute interest he felt in this girl now. He liked the way she sat ; he liked the way she played with her sister ; he liked the way she dug her hands into the sand and threw it in the air. He paused only for a moment to observe the girl. He would have willingly settled there and spent the rest of his life watching her dig her hands into the sand. But that could not be done. There were a lot of people about.

He passed on. He went forward a few paces and

wanted to turn back and take another look at the girl. But that could not be done. He felt that the scores of persons squatting on the sand were all watching him.

He went on his usual walk down to Nallappa's Grove, crossed the river, went up the opposite bank, and away into the fields there ; but he caught himself more than once thinking of the girl. How old was she ? Probably fourteen. Might be even fifteen or sixteen. If she was more than fourteen she must be married. There was a touch of despair in this thought. What was the use of thinking of a married girl ? It would be very improper. He tried to force his mind to think of other things. He tried to engage it in his favourite subject—his trip to England in the coming year. If he was going to England how was he to dress himself ? He had better get used to tie and shoes and coat and hat and knife and fork. He would get a first-class degree in England and come back and marry. What was the use of thinking of a married girl ? Probably she was not married. Her parents were very likely rational and modern, people who abhorred the custom of rushing a young child into marriage. He tried to analyse why he was thinking of her. Why did he think of her so much ? Was it her looks ? Was she so good-looking as all that? Who could say? He hadn't noticed her before. Then how could he say that she was the most beautiful girl in the world? When did he say that? Didn't he? If not, why was he thinking of her so much? Chandran was puzzled, greatly puzzled by the whole thing.

He wondered next what her name might be. She looked like one with the name of Lakshmi. Quite a beautiful name, the name of the Goddess of Wealth, the spouse of God Vishnu, who was the Protector of Creatures.

That night he went home very preoccupied. It was at five o'clock that he had met her, and at nine he was still thinking of her.

After dinner he did not squat on the carpet in the hall, but preferred to go to his room and remain alone there. He tried to read a little; he was in the middle of Wells's *Tono Bungay*. He had found the book gripping, but now he felt it was obtrusive. He was irritated. He put away the book and sat staring at the wall. He presently realized that darkness would be more soothing. He blew out the lamp and sat in his chair. Suppose, though unmarried, she belonged to some other caste? A marriage would not be tolerated even between sub-sects of the same caste. If India was to attain salvation these water-tight divisions must go—Community, Caste, Sects, Sub-sects, and still further divisions. He felt very indignant. He would set an example himself by marrying this girl whatever her caste or sect might be.

The next day he shaved with great care and paid a great deal of attention to his crop, and awaited the evening. When evening came he put on his chocolate-coloured tweed coat and started out. At five he was on the river bank, squatting on the sand near the spot where he had seen the girl the previous day. He sat there for over two hours. The girl did not come. Dozens of other townspeople came to the river and sprawled all over the place, but not that girl. Chandran rose and walked along, peering furtively at every group. It was a very keen search, but it brought forth nothing. Why wasn't she there? His heart beat fast at the sight of every figure that approached the river clad in a *sari*. It was seven forty-five when he set his face homeward, feeling that his brilliantine, shave, ironed tweed coat, were all wasted.

The next day he again went to the river and again waited till seven forty-five in the evening, and went home dispirited. He tossed in bed all night. In moments of half-wakefulness he whispered the word "Lakshmi," "Lakshmi." He suddenly pulled himself up and laughed at himself: it looked as if the girl had paid a first and last visit to the river, and it seemed more than likely that she belonged to another caste, and was married. What a fool he was to go on thinking of her night and day for three whole days. It was a ridiculous obsession. His sobriety ought to assert itself now. An idle brain was the devil's workshop. Too true. A brain given rest for over nine months brought one to this state.

He rose in the morning with a haggard face. His mother asked him if he was not well. Chandran felt that some explanation was due and said he had a terrible headache. His mother, standing two inches shorter than he, put out her hands, stroked his temples, gave him special coffee, and advised him to stay at home the whole day. Chandran felt that nothing could be better than that. He decided not to shave or comb his hair or wear a coat and go out. For he feared that if he went out he might be tempted to go on the foolish quest.

He stayed in his room all day. His father came in at midday and kept him company. He sat in the chair and talked of this and that. Chandran all of a sudden realized that he had better leave Malgudi. That would solve the problem.

"Father, will you let me go to Madras?"

" By all means, if you'd like a change."

" I suppose it will be very hot there ? "

" Must be. The saying is that Madras is hot for ten months in the year and hotter for two."

" Then I don't want to go and fry myself there," said Chandran.

" Try some other place. You can go to your aunt at Bangalore."

" No, no. She will keep telling me what jewels she has got for her daughter. I can't stand her." He decided that he would stay in the best place on earth, home.

Mother came in at about three o'clock to ask how he was feeling. Seenu came in at four-thirty, as soon as school was over, and stood near Chandran's bed, staring at him silently.

" What is it ? " Chandran asked.

" Nothing. Why are you in bed ? "

" Never mind why. What is the news in the school ? "

" We are playing against the Y.M.U on Saturday. After that we are meeting the Board School Eleven. What we can't understand is why the Captain has left out Mohideen. He is bound to have a lot of trouble over that. People are prepared to take it up to the Headmaster."

He could not stay in bed beyond six-thirty. He got up, opened all the windows, washed his face, combed his hair, put on a coat (not the tweed one), and went out. What he needed, he told himself, was plenty of fresh air and exercise and things to think about. Since he wanted exercise he decided to avoid the riverside. The place, he persuaded himself, was stale and crowded. He wished to-day to take a walk at the very opposite end of the town, the Trunk Road. He walked a mile along the Trunk Road and turned back. He hurried back across Lawley Extension, Market Road, and the North Street, and reached the river. It was dark and most people had gone home.

§

Chandran saw her at the river bank next evening. She was wearing a green *sari*, and playing with her little companion. Chandran saw her from a distance and went towards her as if drawn by a rope. But, on approaching her, his courage failed him, and he walked away in the opposite direction. Presently he stopped and blamed himself for wasting a good opportunity of making his person familiar to her; he turned once again with the intention of passing before her closely, slowly, and deliberately. At a distance he could look at her, but when he came close he felt self-conscious and awkward, and while passing actually in front of her he bent his head, fixed his gaze on the ground, and walked fast. He was away, many yards away, from her in a moment. He checked his pace once again and looked back for a fraction of a second, and was quite thrilled at the sight of the green *sari* in the distance. He did not dare to look longer ; for he was obsessed with the feeling that he was being observed by the whole crowd on the river bank. . . . He hoped that she had observed him. He hoped that she had noted his ironed coat. He stood there and debated with himself whether she had seen him or not. One part of him said that she could not have observed him, because he had walked very fast and because there were a lot of people passing and repassing on the sand. Chandran steadily discouraged this sceptical half of his mind, and lent his whole-hearted support to the other half, which was saying that just as he had noticed her in a crowd she was sure to have noticed him. Destiny always worked that way. His well-ironed chocolate tweed was sure to invite notice. He hoped that he didn't walk clumsily in front of her. He again told himself she must have noticed that he was not like the rest of the crowd. And so why should he not now go and occupy a place that would be close to her and in the direct line of her vision? Staring was half the victory in love. His sceptical half now said that by this procedure he might scare her off the river for ever; but, said the other half, to-morrow she may not come to the river at all, and if you don't start an eye friendship immediately, you may not get the opportunity again for a million years. . . . He was engaged in this internal controversy when he received a slap on the back and saw Veeraswami and Mohan, his old class-mates, behind him.

"How are you, Chandran? It seems years since we met."

"We met only last March, less than a year, you know," said Chandran.

Mohan asked, "Chandran, do you remember the evening we spent in your room, reading poetry?"

"Yes, yes. What have you done with your poems?"

"They are still with me."

Chandran felt all his courtesy exhausted. He was not keen on re-unions just then. He tried to get away. But Veeraswami would not let him go: "A year since we met. I have been dying to see an old classmate, and you want to cut me! Won't you come and have a little coffee with us in some restaurant?" He hooked his arm in Chandran's and dragged him along. Chandran tried to resist, and then said, "Let us go this way. I promised to meet somebody. I must see if he is there. . . ." He pointed down the river, past the spot of green *sari*. They went in that direction. Mohan inquired three times what Chandran was doing and received no reply; Veeraswami was talking without a pause. Chandran pretended to listen to him, but constantly turned his head to his left and stole glances at something there; he had to do this without being noticed by his friends. Finally, when he passed before her, he looked at her for so short a space of time that she appeared only as a passing green blur. . . . Before leaving the river bank he looked back twice only. He heartily disliked his companions.

"What are you doing now, Chandran?" Mohan asked, undefeated.

"Nothing at present. I am going to England in a few months."

At this Veeraswami started a heated discourse on the value of going to England. "What have we to learn from the English? I don't know when this craze for going to England will stop. It is a drain on the country's resources. What have we to learn from the English?"

"I may be going there to teach them something," said Chandran. Even granted that she had not noticed him the first time, she couldn't have helped noticing him when he passed before her again; that was why he didn't look at her fully; he didn't want to embarrass her by meeting her gaze.

"Shall we go to the Welcome?" Veeraswami asked.

They had now left the river and were in North Street.

"Anywhere," Chandran said mechanically.

"You seem to be worried over something," Veeraswami said.

"Oh, nothing. I am sorry." Chandran pulled himself up resolutely.

Here were two fellows eager for his company, and he had no business to be absorbed in distant thoughts.

"Forgive me," he said again.

They were now before the Welcome Restaurant, a small, smoky building, from which the smell of sweets and burning ghee assailed the nostrils of passers-by in the street.

They sat round an oily table in the dark hall.

Serving boys were shouting menus and bills and were dashing hither and thither. A server came and asked, " What will you have, sir ? "

" What shall we have ? "

" What will you have ? "

" I want only coffee."

" Have something with it."

" Impossible. Only coffee."

" Bring three cups of coffee, good, strong."

Chandran asked, " What are you doing, Mohan ? Did you get through ? "

" No. I failed, and my uncle cut me. I am now the Malgudi correspondent of the *Daily Messenger* of Madras. They have given me the whole district. They pay me three-eight per column of twenty-one inches."

" Are you making much money ? "

" Sometimes fifty, sometimes ten. It all depends on those rascals, mad fellows. Sometimes they cut everything that I send."

" It is a moderate paper," Veeraswami said jeeringly.

" I am not concerned with their policy," Mohan said.

" What are you doing ? " Chandran asked, turning to Veeraswami.

" It will take a whole day for me to tell you. I am starting a movement called the Resurrection Brigade. I am touring about a lot on that business."

" What is the brigade ? "

" It is only an attempt to prepare the country for revolution. Montagu-Chelmsford reform, Simon Report, and what not, are all a fraud. Our politicians, including the Congressmen, are playing into the hands of the Imperialists. The Civil Disobedience Movement is a childish business. Our brigade will gain the salvation of our country by an original method. Will you join it ? Mohan is already a member."

Chandran promised to think it over, and asked what they expected Mohan to do for the movement.

" Everything. We want everybody there, poets, philosophers, musicians, sculptors, and swordsmen."

" What is its strength now ? "

" About twenty-five have so far signed the brigade pledge. I expect that in two years we shall have a membership of fifty thousand in South India alone."

They finished their coffee and rose. They went back to the river, smoked cigarettes, and talked all the evening. Before parting, Chandran promised to see them again and asked them where they lived.

" I am staying with Mohan," said Veeraswami.

"Where do you live, Mohan?"

"Room 14, Modern Indian Lodge, Mill Street."

"Right. I shall drop in sometime," said Chandran.

"I won't be in town after Tuesday. I am going into the country for six months," said Veeraswami.

§

Chandran realized that friends and acquaintances were likely to prove a nuisance to him by the river. He decided to cut every one hereafter. With this resolution he went to the Sarayu bank next evening. He also decided to be very bold, and indifferent to the public's observation and criticism.

She was there with her little companion.

Chandran went straight to a spot just thirty yards from where she sat, and settled down there. He had determined to stare at her this evening. He might even throw in an elegant wink or smile. He was going to stare at her and take in a lot of details regarding her features. He had not made out yet whether she was fair or light brown; whether she had long hair or short, and whether her eyes were round or almond-shaped; and he had also some doubts about her nose.

He sat at this thirty yards range and kept throwing

at her a side glance every fifth second. He noticed that she played a great deal with her little companion. He wanted to go to her and ask whether the little companion was her sister or cousin and how old she was. But he abandoned the idea. A man of twenty-two going up and conversing with a grown-up girl, a perfect stranger, would be affording a very uncommon sight to the public.

§

This optical communion became a daily habit. His powers of observation and deduction increased tremendously. He gathered several facts about the girl. She wore a dark *sari* and a green *sari* alternately. She came to the river chiefly for the sake of her little companion. She was invariably absent on Fridays and came late on Wednesdays. Chandran concluded from this that the girl went to the temple on Friday evenings, and was delayed by a music master or a stitching master on Wednesdays. He further gathered that she was of a religious disposition, and was accomplished in the art of music or embroidery. From her regularity he concluded that she was a person of very systematic habits. The fact that she played with her young companion showed that she had a loving disposition. He concluded that she had no brothers, since not a single soul escorted her on any evening. Encouraged by this conclusion, he wondered if he should not stop her and talk to her when she rose to go home. He might even accompany her to her house. That might become a beautiful habit. What wonderful things he would have to say to her. When the traffic of the town had died, they could walk together under the moon or in magic starlight. He would stop a few yards from her house. What a parting of sweetness and pain ! . . . It must be noted that in this dream the young companion did not exist, or, if she did, she came to the river and went home all by herself.

An evening of this optical fulfilment filled him with tranquillity. He left the river and went home late in the evening, meditating on God, and praying to Him with concentration that He would bless this romance with success. All night he repeated her name, " Lakshmi," and fervently hoped that her soul heard his call through the night.

§

He had lived for over a month in a state of bliss, notwithstanding his ignorance. He began to feel now that he ought to be up and doing and get a little more practical. He could not go on staring at her on the sands all his life. He must know all about her.

He followed her at a distance of about half a furlong on a dark evening when she returned home from the river. He saw her enter a house in Mill Street. He paced before the house slowly, twice, slowing up to see if there was any board before the house. There was none.

He remembered suddenly that Mohan lived in Mill Street. Room number 14, Modern Indian Lodge, he had said. He went up and down the street in search of the hotel. At last he found it was the building opposite the girl's house. There was a signboard, but that could not be seen in the dark. Room number 14 was half a cubicle on the staircase landing. The cubicle was divided by a high wooden partition into Room 14 and Room 15.

Mohan was delighted to receive Chandran.

" Is Veeraswami gone ? " Chandran asked.

" Weeks ago," replied Mohan.

There was not a single table or chair in the room. Mohan lived on a striped carpet spread on the floor. He sat on it reclining against the wooden partition. There was a yellow trunk in a corner of the room, on which a shining nickel flower vase was kept with some paper flowers in it. The room received its light and ventilation from the single window in Room 15, over the wooden partition. A bright gas lamp hung over the wooden partition and shed its greenish glare impartially on Room 14 and Room 15.

"Would you believe it? I have never been in this street before," said Chandran.

"Indeed! But why should you come here? You live at the south end while this is the east end of the town."

"I like this street," Chandran said. "I wonder why this is called Mill Street. Are all the people that live here mill owners?"

"Nothing of the kind. Years ago there were two weaving mills at the end of the street. There are all sorts of people here."

"Oh. Any particularly important person?"

"None that I can think of."

It was on Chandran's lips, at this point, to ask who lived in the opposite house. But he merely said that he wished to meet his friend oftener in his room.

"I go out news-hunting at ten in the morning and return at about four, after posting my letters. I do not usually go out after that. You can come any time you please," said Mohan.

"Have you no holidays?"

"On Sundays we have no paper. And so on Saturday I have a holiday. I spend the whole day in the room. Please do come any time you like, and as often as you like."

"Thanks, thanks. I have absolutely no company. I shall be delighted to come here frequently."

CHAPTER EIGHT

§

THROUGH Mohan's co-operation Chandran learnt that his sweetheart's name was Malathi, that she was unmarried, and that she was the daughter of Mr. D. W. Krishna Iyer, Head Clerk in the Executive Engineer's office.

The suffix to the name of the girl's father was a comforting indication that he was of the same caste and sub-caste as Chandran. Chandran shuddered at the thought of all the complications that he would have had to face if the gentleman had been Krishna Iyengar, or Krishna Rao, or Krishna Mudaliar. His father would certainly cast him off if he tried to marry out of caste.

Chandran took it all as a favourable sign, as an answer to his prayers, which were growing intenser every day. In each fact, that Mohan lived in the hotel opposite her house, that she was unmarried, that her father was an "Iyer," Chandran felt that God was revealing Himself.

Chandran prayed to God to give him courage, and went to his father to talk to him about his marriage. His courage failed him at the last moment, and he went away after discussing some fatuous subject. The next day he again went to his father with the same resolution and again lapsed into fatuity. He went back to his room and regretted his cowardice. He would be unworthy of Malathi if he was going to be such a spineless worm. Afraid of a father! He was not a baby asking for a toy, but a full-grown adult out on serious business, very serious business. It was very doubtful if a squirming coward would be any good to Malathi as a husband.

He went back to his father, who was on the veranda reading something. Mother had gone out to see some friends; Seenu had gone to school. This was the best time to talk to Father confidentially.

Father put down the book on seeing Chandran, and pulled the spectacles from over his nose. Chandran drew a chair close to Father's easy-chair.

"Have you read this book, Chandar?"

Chandran looked at it—some old novel, Dickens. "No." At another time he would have added, "I hate Dickens's laborious humour," and involved himself in a debate. But now he merely said, "I will try to read it later." He did not want to throw away precious time in literary discussions.

"Father, please don't mistake me. I want to marry D. W. Krishna Iyer's daughter."

Father put on his spectacles and looked at his son with a frown. He sat up and asked, "Who is he?"

"Head Clerk in the Executive Engineer's office."

"Why do you want to marry his daughter?"

"I like her."

"Do you know the girl?"

"Yes. I have seen her often."

"Where?"

Chandran told him.

"Have you spoken to each other?"

"No. . . ."

"Does she know you?"

"I don't know."

Father laughed, and it cut into Chandran's soul.

Father asked, "In that case why this girl alone and not any other?"

Chandran said, "I like her," and left Father's company abruptly as Father said, "I don't know anything about these things. I must speak to your mother."

Later Mother came into Chandran's room and asked, "What is all this?" Chandran answered with an insolent silence.

"Who is this girl?" There was great anxiety in her voice.

Chandran told her. She was very disappointed. A Head Clerk's daughter was not what she had hoped to get for her son. "Chandar, why won't you consider any of the dozens of girls that have been proposed to you?"

Chandran rejected this suggestion indignantly.

"But suppose those girls are richer and more beautiful?"

"I don't care. I shall marry this girl and no one else."

"But how are you sure they are prepared to give their daughter to you?"

"They will have to."

"Extraordinary! Do you think marriage is a child's game? We don't know anything about them, who they are, what they are, what they are worth, if the stars and the other things about the girl are all right, and above all, whether they are prepared to marry their girl at all. . . ."

"They will have to. I hear that this season she will be married because she is getting on for sixteen."

"Sixteen!" Mother screamed. "They can't be all right if they have kept the girl unmarried till sixteen. She must have attained puberty ages ago.

They can't be all right. We have a face to keep in this town. Do you think it is all child's play ?"
She left the room in a temper.

§

In a few days this hostility had to be abandoned, because Chandran's parents could not bear for long the sight of an unhappy Chandran. For his sake they were prepared to compromise to this extent : they were prepared to consider the proposal if it came from the other side. Whatever happened they would not take the initiative in the matter ; for they belonged to the bridegroom's side, and according to time-honoured practice it was the bride's people who proposed first. Anything done contrary to this would make them the laughing-stock of the community.

Chandran raved : "To the dust-pot with your silly customs."

But his mother replied that she at any rate belonged to a generation which was in no way worse than the present one for all its observances ; and as long as she lived she would insist on respecting the old customs. Ordinary talk at home was becoming rarer every day. It was always a debate on Custom and

Reason. His father usually remained quiet during these debates. One of the major mysteries in life for Chandran at this period was the question as to which side his father favoured. He did not appear to place active obstacles in Chandran's way, but he did little else. He appeared to distrust his own wisdom in these matters and to have handed the full rein to his wife. Chandran once or twice tried to sound him and gain him to his side ; but he was evasive and non-committal.

Chandran's only support and consolation at this juncture was Mohan. To his room he went every night after dinner. This visit was not entirely from an unmixed motive. While on his way he could tarry for a while before her house and gladden his heart with a sight of her under the hall-lamp as she passed from one part of the house to another. Probably she was going to bed ; blessed be those pillows. Or probably she went in and read ; ah, blessed books with the touch of her hands on them. He would often speculate what hour she would go to bed, what hour she would rise, and how she lay down and slept and how her bed looked. Could he not just dash into the house, hide in the passage, steal up to her bed at night, crush her in his arms, and carry her away ?

If it happened to be late, and the lights in the house were put out, he would walk distractedly up and down before the house, and then go to Room 14 of the Modern Indian Lodge.

Mohan would put away whatever poem he was writing. But for him Chandran would have been shrivelled up by the heat of a hopeless love. Mohan would put away his pad, and clear a space on the carpet for Chandran.

Chandran would give him the latest bulletin from the battle front, and then pass on to a discussion of theories.

" If the girl's father were called something other than a Head Clerk, and given a hundred more to his pay, I am sure your parents would move heaven and earth to secure this alliance," said the poet.

" Why should we be cudgelled and nose-led by our elders ? " Chandran asked indignantly. " Why can't we be allowed to arrange our lives as we please ? Why can't they leave us to rise or sink on our own ideals ? "

These were mighty questions ; and the poet tackled them in his own way. " Money is the greatest god in life. Father and mother and brother do not care for anything but your money. Give them money and they will leave you alone. I am just writing a few lines entitled " Moneylove." It is free verse. You must hear it. I have dedicated it to you." Mohan picked up the pad and read :

" The parents loved you, you thought.
No, no, not you, my dear.
They've loved nothing less for its own sake.
They fed you and petted you and pampered you
Because some day they hope you will bring them
money ;
Much money, so much and more and still more ;
Because some day, they hope, you'll earn a
Bride who'll bring much money, so much and
More and still more. . . ."

There were two more stanzas in the same strain. It brought the tears to Chandran's eyes. He hated his father and mother. He took this poem with him when he went home.

He gave it to his father next day. Father read through it twice and asked with a dry smile : " Did you write this ? "

" Never mind the authorship," Chandran said.

" Do you believe what these lines say ? "

" I do," said Chandran, and did not stay there for further talk.

When he was gone Father explained the poem to Mother, who began to cry. Father calmed her and said, "This is what he seems to feel. I don't know what to do."

"We have promised to consider it if it is made from that side. What more can we do?"

"I don't know."

"They seem to be thorough rogues. The marriage season has already begun. Why can't they approach us? They expect Chandran to go to them, touch their feet, and beg them for their girl."

"They probably do not know that Chandran is available," said Father.

"Why do you defend them? They can't be ignorant of the existence of a possible bridegroom like Chandran. That man, the girl's father, seems to be a deep man. He is playing a deep game. He is waiting for our boy to go to him, when he can get a good husband for his daughter without giving a dowry and without an expensive wedding. . . . This boy Chandra is talking nonsense. This is what we get from our children for all our troubles. . . . I am in a mood to let him do anything he likes. . . . But what more can we do? I shall drown myself in Sarayu before I allow any proposal to go from here."

CHAPTER NINE

§

CHANDRAN'S parents sent for Ganapathi Sastrigal, who was match-maker in general to a few important families in Malgudi. He had a small income from his lands in the village; he was once a third clerk in a Collector's Office, which also gave him now a two-digit pension. After retiring from Government service he settled down as a general adviser, officiating priest at rituals, and a match-maker. He confined his activities to a few rich families in the town.

He came next day in the hot sun, and went straight into the kitchen, where Chandran's mother was preparing some sweets.

"Oh, come in, come in," Chandran's mother exclaimed on seeing him. "Why have you been neglecting us so long? It is over a year since you came to our house."

"I had to spend some months in the village.

There was some dispute about the lands ; and also some arrears had to be collected from the tenants. I tell you lands are a curse. . . ."

"Oh, you are standing," she cried, and said to the cook, "Take a sitting-board and give it to him."

"No, no, no. Don't trouble yourself. I can sit on the floor," said the old man. He received the proffered sitting board, but gently put it away and sat on the floor.

"Won't you take a little tiffin and coffee ?" Chandran's mother asked.

"Oh, no. Don't trouble yourself. I have just had it all in my house. Don't trouble yourself."

"Absolutely no trouble," she said, and set before him a plate of sweets and a tumbler of coffee.

He ate the sweets slowly, and poured the coffee down his throat, holding the tumbler high over his lips. He said, "I have taken this because you have put it before me, and I don't like to see anything wasted. My digestion is not as good as it was before I had the jaundice. I recently showed myself to a doctor, Doctor Kesavan. I wonder if you know him ? He is the son-in-law of Raju of Trichinopoly, whom I have known since his boyhood. The doctor said that I must give up tamarind and use only lemon in its place. . . ."

Afterwards he followed her out of the kitchen to the back veranda of the house. Chandran's mother spread a mat before him and requested him to sit on it, and opened the subject.

"Do you know D. W. Krishna Iyer's family?"

The old man sat thinking for a while, and then said, "D. W. Krishnan; you mean Coimbatore Appaji's nephew, the fellow who is in the Executive Engineer's office? I have known their family for three generations."

"I am told that he has a daughter ready for marriage."

The old man remained very thoughtful and said, "Yes, it is true. He has a daughter old enough to have a son, but not yet married."

"Why is it so? Anything wrong with the family?"

"Absolutely nothing," replied the old man. He now saw he ought not to be critical in his remarks. He tried to mend his previous statement. "Absolutely nothing. Any one that says such a thing will have a rotting tongue. The girl is only well-grown, and I don't think she is as old as she looks. She can't be more than fifteen. This has become the standard age for girls nowadays. Everybody holds advanced views in these days. Even in an ancient and orthodox family like Sadasiva Iyer's they married a girl recently at fifteen ! "

This was very comforting to Chandran's mother. She asked, " Do you think that it is a good family ? "

" D. W. Krishnan comes of a very noble family. His father was . . ." The Sastrigal went on giving an impressive history of the family, ranging over three generations. " If Krishnan is now only a Head Clerk it is because when he came into the property his elder brothers had squandered all of it and left only debts and encumbrances. Krishnan was rocked in a golden cradle when he was young, but became the foster-son of Misfortune after his father died. It is all fate. Who can foresee what is going to happen ? "

After two hours of talk he left the house on a mission ; that was to go to D. W. Krishna Iyer's house and ascertain if they were going to marry their girl this season, and to move them to take the initiative in a proposal for an alliance with Chandran's family. The old man was to give out that he was acting independently, and on his own initiative.

§

Next day Ganapathi Sastrigal came with good news. As soon as Chandran's mother saw him at the gate she cried, " Sastrigal has come ! "

As soon as he climbed the veranda steps Chandran's father said, " Ah, come in, come in, Sastriar," and pushed a chair towards him. The Sastrigal sat on the edge of the chair, wiped the sweat off his nape with his upper cloth, and said to Mother, " Summer has started very early this year. . . . Do you cool water in a mud jug ? "

" Certainly, otherwise it is impossible to quench our thirst in summer. It is indispensable."

" If that is so, please ask your cook to bring me a tumbler of jug water."

" You must drink some coffee."

" Don't trouble yourself. Water will do."

" Will you take a little tiffin ? "

" No, no. Give me only water. Don't trouble yourself about coffee or tiffin."

" Absolutely no trouble," said Mother, and went in and returned with a tumbler of coffee.

" You are putting yourself to great trouble bringing me this coffee," said the old man, taking the tumbler.

"Have you any news for us?" she asked.

"Plenty, plenty," said the old man. "I went to D. W. Krishnan's house this morning; as you may already know, we have known each other for three generations. He was not at home when I went. He had gone to see his officer or on some such work, but his wife was there. She asked her daughter to spread a mat for me, and then sent her in to bring me coffee. I am simply filled with coffee everywhere. I drank the coffee and gave the tumbler back to the girl. . . . She is a smart girl; stands very tall, and has a good figure. Her skin is fair, may be called fair, though not as fair as that of our lady here; but she is by no means to be classed as a dark girl. Her mother says that the girl has just completed her fourteenth year." Chandran's mother felt a great load off her mind now. She wouldn't have to marry her son to a girl over sixteen, and incur the comments of the community.

"I knew all along that there couldn't be truth in what people said . . ." she said.

"And then we talked of one thing and another," said the Sastrigal, "and the subject came to marriage. You can take it from me that they are going to marry their girl this season. She will certainly be married in *Panguni* month. Just as I was thinking of going,

Krishnan came in. He is a very good fellow. He showed me the regard due to my age, and due to me for my friendship with his father and uncles. He is very eager to complete the marriage this season. He asked me to help him to secure a bridegroom. I suggested two or three others and then your son. I may tell you that he thinks he will be extraordinarily blessed if he can secure an alliance with your family. He feels you may not stoop to his status."

"Status! Status!" Chandran's mother exclaimed. "We have seen with these very eyes people who were rich once, but are in the streets now, and such pranks of fate. What a foolish notion to measure status with money. It is here to-day and gone to-morrow. What I would personally care for most in any alliance would be character and integrity."

"That I can guarantee," said the Sastrigal. "When I mentioned this family, the lady was greatly elated. She seems to know you all very well. She even said that she and you were related. It seems that your maternal grandfather's first wife and her paternal grandfather were sister and brother, not cousins, but direct sister and brother."

"Ah, I did not know that. I am so happy to hear it." She then asked, "Have you any idea how much they are prepared to spend?"

"Yes. I got it out in a manner ; very broadly, of course ; but that will do for the present. I think they are prepared to give a cash dowry of about two thousand rupees, silver vessels and presents up to a thousand, and spend about a thousand on the wedding celebrations. These will be in addition to about a thousand worth of diamond and gold on the girl."

Chandran's mother was slightly disappointed at the figures. "We can settle all that later."

"Quite right," said the old man. "To-morrow, if everything is auspicious, they will send you the girl's horoscope. We shall proceed with the other matters after comparing the horoscopes. I am certain that this marriage will take place very soon. Even as I started for their house a man came bearing pots of foaming toddy ; it is an excellent omen. I am certain that this alliance will be completed."

"Why bother with horoscopes ?" asked Chandran's father. "Personally, I have no faith in them."

"You must not say that," said the Sastrigal. "How are we to know whether two persons brought together will have health, happiness, harmony, and long life, if we do not study their horoscopes individually and together ?"

§

Chandran felt very happy that her horoscope was coming. He imagined that the very next thing after the horoscope would be marriage. The very fact that they were willing to send the girl's horoscope for comparison proved that they were not averse to this alliance. They were probably goaded on by the girl. He had every reason to believe that the girl had told her parents she would marry Chandran and no one else. But how could she know him or his name ? Girls had a knack of learning of these things by a sort of sixth sense. How splendid of her to speak out her mind like this, brave girl. If her mind matched her form, it must be one of the grandest things in the world. . . .

The thought of her melted him. He clutched his pillow and cried in the darkness, " Darling, what are you doing ? Do you hear me ? "

In these days he met her less often at the river, but he made it up by going to Mill Street and wandering in front of her house until her form passed under the hall light. He put down her absence at the river to her desire to save Chandran's reputation. She felt, Chandran thought, that seeing him every day at the river would give rise to gossip. Such a selfless creature. Would rather sacrifice her evening's outing than subject Chandran to gossip. Chandran had no doubt that she was going to be the most perfect wife a man could ever hope to get.

As he sauntered in front of her house, Chandran would often ask God when His grace would bend low so that Chandran might cease to be a man in the street and stride into the house as a son-in-law. After they were married, he would tell her everything. They would sit in their creeper-covered villa on the hill slope, just those two, and watch the sun set. In the afterglow of the evening he would tell her of his travails, and they would both laugh.

The next day Ganapathi Sastrigal did not come, and Chandran began to think wild things. What was the matter? Had they suddenly backed out?

The horoscope was not sent on the next day either. Chandran asked his mother every half-hour if it had come, and finally suggested that some one should be sent to bring it. When this suggestion reached Father's ears, he asked, "Why don't you yourself go and ask them for a copy of the girl's horoscope?"

Chandran's mind being in a state of lowered efficiency, he asked eagerly, "Shall I? I thought I shouldn't do it."

Father laughed and told it to Mother, who became scared and said, " Chandra, please don't do it. It would be a very curious procedure. They will send the horoscope themselves."

Father said to Chandran, " Look here, you will never be qualified to marry unless you cultivate a lot of patience. It is the only power that you will be allowed to exercise when you are married."

Mother looked at Father suspiciously and said, " Will you kindly make your meaning clearer ? "

Chandran went to his room in a very distracted state. He tried to read a novel, but his mind kept wandering. Seenu, his younger brother, came in and asked, " Brother, are you not well ? " He could not understand what was wrong with Chandran. He very much missed Chandran's company in the after-dinner chatting group ; he very much missed his supervision, though it had always been aggressive. Chandran looked at him without giving any answer. Seenu wanted to ask if his brother was about to be married, but he was too shy to mention a thing like marriage. So he asked if Chandran was unwell. Chandran answered, after the question was repeated, " I am quite well ; why ? "

" You don't look well."

" Quite likely."

"That is all I wanted to know. Because Mother said that you were going to be married."

There was no obvious connection between the two, but Seenu felt he had led on to the delicate topic with cunning diplomacy.

Chandran asked, "Boy, would you like to have a sister-in-law?"

Seenu slunk behind the chair with shame at this question.

Chandran made it worse by asking, "Would you like a sister-in-law to be called Malathi?"

At this Seenu was so abashed that he ran out of the room, leaving Chandran to the torture of his thoughts and worries.

§

When the horoscope did not come on the next day, Chandran went to Mohan and asked, "Why should I not go to Mr. Krishna Iyer and ask for it?"

Mohan replied, "Why have you not done it already?"

"I thought that it might be irregular."

"Would it be different now?"

Chandran remained silent. His special pride in the conducting of his romance so far was that he had not committed the slightest irregularity at any time. He felt that he could easily have talked to her when she was alone on the sands ; he could have tried to write to her ; he could have befriended Mr. Krishna Iyer and asked him for the hand of his daughter ; and he could have done a number of other things, but he didn't, for the sake of his parents ; he wanted everything to be done in the correct, orthodox manner.

Mohan said, " I don't care for orthodoxy and correctness myself. But since you care for those things, at least for the sake of your parents keep it up and don't do anything rashly now."

But Chandran wailed that they had not sent the horoscope. What could it mean except coldness on their part ?

Mohan said, " Till they show some more solid proof of their coldness we ought not to do anything."

Chandran rested in gloom for a while and then came out with a bright idea : " I have got to know the girl's father, and you must help me."

" How ? "

" You are a newspaper correspondent, and you have access everywhere. Why don't you go to his house on some work ; say that you want some news connected with the Engineering Department. People are awfully nice to newspaper correspondents."

"They are. But where do you come in?"

"You can take me along with you and introduce me to him. You may even say that I am your assistant."

"How is that going to help you?"

"You had better leave that to me."

"There is absolutely no excuse for me to go and see him."

"There is a rumour of a bridge over Sarayu, near Nallappa's Grove. You must know if it is true. Engineering Department." Mohan realized that love sharpened the wits extraordinarily.

While walking home Chandran formulated a perfect scheme for interviewing Mr. D. W. Krishna Iyer. He would do it without Mohan's help. The scheme that he had suggested to Mohan fired his imagination. Chandran decided to go and knock on the door of Krishna Iyer's house. Malathi would open the door. He would ask her if her father was in, and tell her he was there in order to know if it was a fact that there was going to be a bridge over Sarayu; he could tell her he would call in again and go away. This would help him to see her at close quarters, and to decide once for all whether her eyes were round or almond-shaped, and whether her complexion was light brown or dusky translucence. He might even carry a small camera with him and take a snapshot of her. For one of the major exercises for his mind at that time was trying to recollect the features of Malathi, which constantly dissolved and tormented him. His latest hobby was scanning the faces of passers-by in the streets to see if any one resembled her. She had no double in the world. There was a boy in a wayside shop whose arched, dark eyebrows seemed to Chandran to resemble Malathi's ; Chandran often went to that shop and bought three-pies worth of peppermint and gazed at the boy's eyebrows.

There was good news for him at home. Ganapathi Sastrigal came in the evening with the girl's horoscope. He explained that the delay was due to the fact that the preceding days were inauspicious. He took Chandran's horoscope with him, to give to the girl's people.

So the first courtesies were exchanged between the families. As Chandran looked at the small piece of paper on which the horoscope was drawn, his heart bubbled over with joy. He noticed that the corners of the paper were touched with saffron—a mark of auspiciousness. So they had fully realized that it was an auspicious undertaking. Did not that fact indicate that they approved of this bridegroom and were anxious to secure him? If they were anxious to secure him, did not that mean that she would soon be his? Chandran read the horoscope a number of times, though he understood very little of it. It dissipated his accumulated gloom in a moment.

Chandran was very happy the whole of the next day; but his mother constantly checked his exuberance: "Chandra, you must not think that the only thing now to be settled is the date of the marriage. God helping, all the difficulties will be solved, but there are yet a number of preliminaries to be settled. First, our astrologer must tell us if your horoscope can be matched with the girl's; and then I don't know what their astrologer will say. Let us hope for the best. After that, they must come and invite us to see the girl."

"I have seen the girl, Mother, and I like her."

"All the same they must invite us, and we must go there formally. After that they must come and ask us if you like the girl. And the terms of the marriage must be discussed and settled. . . . I don't mean to discourage you, but you must be patient till all this is settled."

Chandran sat biting his nails: "But, Mother, you won't create difficulties over the dowry ?"

"We shall see. We must not be too exacting, nor can we cheapen ourselves."

"But suppose you haggle too much ?"

"Don't you worry about anything, boy. If they won't give you the girl on reasonable conditions, I shall get you other girls a thousand times more suitable."

"Don't talk like that, Mother. I shall never forgive you if this marriage does not take place through your bickerings over the dowry and the presents."

"We have a status and a prestige to keep. We can't lower ourselves unduly."

"You care more for your status than for the happiness of your son."

"It doesn't seem proper for you to be speaking like this, Chandra."

Chandran argued and tried to prove that demanding a cash dowry amounted to extortion. He said that the bridegroom's parents exploited the anxiety of the parents of a girl, who must be married before she attained puberty. This kind of talk always irritated Chandran's mother. She said, "My father gave seven thousand in cash to your father, and over two thousand in silver vessels, and spent nearly five thousand on wedding celebrations. What was wrong in it? How are we any the worse for it? It is the duty of every father to set some money apart for securing a son-in-law. We can't disregard custom."

Chandran said that it was all irrational extravagance and that the total expenses for a marriage ought not to exceed a hundred rupees.

"You may go and tell your girl's father that, and finish your marriage and come home. I shall gladly receive you and your wife, but don't expect any of us to attend the wedding. If you want us there, everything must be done in the proper manner."

"But, Mother," Chandran pleaded, "you will be reasonable in your demands, won't you? They are not well-to-do."

"We shall see; but don't try to play their lawyer already. Time enough for that."

Father was dressing to go out. Chandran went to him and reported his mother's attitude. Father said, "Don't be frightened. She doesn't mean you any harm."

"But suppose she holds to a big dowry and they can't pay. What is to happen?"

"Well, well, there is time to think of that yet.

They have taken your horoscope. Let them come and tell us what they think of the horoscopes."

He took his walking-stick and started out. Chandran followed him to the gate, pleading. He wanted his father to stop and assure him of his support against Mother.

But Father merely said, " Don't worry," and went out.

CHAPTER TEN

§

THREE days later a peon from the Engineering Department came with a letter for Father. Father, who was on the veranda, took it, and after reading it, passed it on to Chandran, who was sitting in a chair with a book. The letter read :

"DEAR AND RESPECTED SIR,—I am returning herewith the copy of your son's horoscope, which you so kindly sent to me for comparison with my daughter's. Our family astrologer, after careful study and comparison, says that the horoscopes cannot be matched. Since I have great faith in horoscopy, and since I have known from experience that the marriage of couples ill-matched in the stars often leads to misfortune and even tragedy, I have to seek a bridegroom elsewhere. I hope that your honoured self, your wife, and your son will forgive me for the unnecessary trouble I have caused you. No one can have a greater regret at missing an alliance with your family than I. However, we can only propose. He on the Thirupathi Hills alone knows what is best for us.

"With regards,

"Yours sincerely,

"D. W. Krishnan."

Chandran gave the letter back to his father, rose without a word, and went to his room. Father sat tapping the envelope on his left hand, and called his wife.

"Here they have written that the horoscopes don't match."

"Have they? . . . H'm. I knew all along that they were up to some such trick. If there is any flaw in the horoscope it must be in the girl's, not in the boy's. His is a first-class horoscope. They want a cheap bridegroom, somebody who will be content with a dowry of one hundred rupees and a day's celebration of the wedding, and they know that they cannot get Chandra on those terms. They want some excuse to back out now." She remained silent for a while, and said, "So much the better. I have always disliked this proposal to tack Chandran on to a hefty, middle-aged girl. There are fifty girls waiting to be married to him."

Just when Father was dressed and ready to go out, Chandran came out of his room and said in a voice that was thick, " Father, will you still try and find out if something can't be done ? "

Father was about to answer, " Don't worry about this girl, I shall get you another girl," but he looked up and saw that Chandran's eyes were red. So he said, " Don't worry. I shall find out what is wrong and try to set it right." He went out, and Chandran went back to his room and bolted the door.

Chandran's father wrote next day :

> " DEAR MR. KRISHNAN,—I shall be very glad if you will kindly come and see me this evening. I meant to call on you, but I did not know what hour would suit you. Since I am always free, I shall be at your service and await the pleasure of meeting you."

Mr. Krishna Iyer came that evening. After the courtesies of coffee and inane inquiries were over, Chandran's father asked, " Now, sir, please tell me why the horoscopes don't match."

" I ought not to be saying it, sir, but there is a flaw in your son's horoscope. Our astrologer has found that the horoscopes cannot be matched. If my girl's horoscope had Moon or Mars in the Seventh

House, there couldn't be a better match than your son for her. But as it is . . ."

" Are you sure ? "

" I know a little of astrology myself. I am prepared to overlook many things in a horoscope. I don't usually concern myself with the factors that indicate prosperity, wealth, progeny, and all that. I usually overlook them. But I do feel that we can't ignore the question of longevity. I know hundreds of cases where the presence of Mars in this house . . . I can tell you that . . ." He hesitated to say it. " It kills the wife soon after the marriage," he said, when pressed by Chandran's father.

Chandran's father was for dropping the question at this point, but when he remembered that Chandran had shut himself in his room, he sent for one Srouthigal, an eminent astrologer and almanac-compiler in the town.

The next day there was a conference over the question of the stars and their potency. After four hours of intricate calculations and the filling of several sheets of paper with figures, Srouthigal said that there was nothing wrong with Chandran's horoscope. D. W. Krishna Iyer was sent for, and he came. Srouthigal looked at Krishna Iyer and said, " These two horoscopes are well matched."

"Did you notice the Mars?"

"Yes, but it is powerless now. It is now under the sway of the Sun, which looks at it from the Fifth House."

"But I doubt it, sir," Krishna Iyer said.

Srouthigal thrust the papers into Krishna Iyer's hands, and asked, "How old is the boy?"

"Nearly twenty-three."

"What is twelve and eight?"

"Twenty."

"How can the boy be affected by it at twenty-three. If he had married at twenty, he might have had to marry again, but not now. Mars became powerless when the boy was twenty years, three months, and five days old."

"But I get it differently in my calculations," said Krishna Iyer. "The power of Mars lasts till the boy reaches twenty-five years and eight months."

"Which almanac do you follow?" asked Srouthigal, with a fiery look.

"The *Vakya*," said Krishna Iyer.

"There you are," said Srouthigal. "Why don't you base your calculations on the *Drig* almanac?"

"From time immemorial we have followed only the *Vakya*, and nothing has gone wrong so far. I think it is the only true almanac."

"You are making a very strange statement," said the Srouthigal, with a sneer.

When he went home Krishna Iyer took the papers with him, promising to calculate again and reconsider. He wrote to Chandran's father next day: "I worked all night, till about 4 a.m., on the horoscopes. Our astrologer was also with me. We have not arrived at any substantially different results now. The only change we find is that the Sun's sway comes in the boy's twenty-fifth year and fourth month and not in the eighth month as I stated previously.

"Any one who is not a fanatic of the *Drig* system will see that the potency of Mars lasts very nearly till the boy's twenty-fifth year. This is not a matter in which we can take risks. It is a question of life and death to a girl. Mars has never been known to spare. He kills.

"I seek your forgiveness for all the trouble I may have caused you in this business. I cannot find adequate words to express how unhappy I am to miss the opportunity of an alliance with your great house. I hope God will bless Mr. Chandran with a suitable bride soon. . . ."

Chandran's mother raved, "Why can't you leave these creatures alone? A black dot on Chandran's horoscope is what we get for associating with them. If they go on spreading the rumour that Chandran has Mars, a nice chance he will have of ever getting a girl. This is what we get for trying to pick up something from a gutter."

When she was gone, Chandran suggested to his father, "Let us grant that Mars lasts till my twenty-fifth year. I am nearly twenty-three now. I shall be twenty-five very soon. Why don't you tell them that I will wait till my twenty-fifth year; let them also wait for two years. Let us come to an understanding with them."

Chandran's father knew that it would be perfectly useless to reason things with Chandran. Hence he said that he would try to meet Krishna Iyer and suggest this to him.

Thereafter every day Chandran privately asked his father if he had met Krishna Iyer, and Father gave the stock reply that Krishna Iyer could not be found either at home or in his office.

§

After waiting for a few days Chandran wrote a letter to Malathi. He guarded against making it a love letter. It was, according to Chandran's belief, a simple, matter-of-fact piece of writing. It only contained an account of his love for her. It explained to her the difficulty in the horoscope, and asked her if she was prepared to wait for him for two years. Let her write the single word " Yes " or " No " on a piece of paper and post it to him. He enclosed a stamped addressed envelope for a reply.

He took the letter to Mohan and said, " This is my last chance."

" What is this ? "

" It is a letter to her."

" Oh, God ! You can't do that ! "

" It is not a love letter. It is a dry, business letter. You must see that it is somehow delivered to her."

" Have I to wait for a reply ? "

" No. She can post a reply. I have arranged for it."

" They will shoo me out if they see me delivering a letter to a grown-up girl."

" But you must somehow manage it for my sake. This is my last attempt. I shall wait till I receive a reply . . ." said Chandran, and completed the sentence in sobs.

Next morning he went to the post office and asked the Lawley Extension postman if there was any letter for him. This became a daily routine. Day followed day thus. He rarely went to the river now. He avoided going to the Modern Indian Lodge because it was opposite to her house.

On an evening, a fortnight later, Chandran started for the Modern Indian Lodge. "I must grit my teeth and pass before her house, go to the hotel, see Mohan, and ask him why there is no letter yet," he told himself.

When he came to Mill Street he heard a drum and pipe music. His heart beat fast. When he reached the Modern Indian Lodge he saw that the entrance of the opposite house was decorated with plantain stems and festoons of mango leaves. These were marks of an auspicious event. Chandran's body trembled. The drummer, sitting on the pyol in front of the house, beat the drum with all the vigour in his arms ; the piper was working a crescendo in *Kalyani raga*. The music scalded Chandran's ears. He ran up the steps to Mohan's room.

"What are they doing in the opposite house ?"

Mohan sprang up, put his arms around Chandran, and soothed him, "Calm yourself. This won't do."

Chandran shouted, "What are they doing in the opposite house ? Tell me ! Why this pipe, why the mango leaves, who is going to be married in that house ?"

"Nobody yet, but presently. They are celebrating the Wedding Notice. I learn that she is to marry her cousin next week."

"What has happened to my letter?"

"I don't know."

"Will nobody choke that piper? He is murdering the tune."

"Sit down, Chandran."

"Did you deliver that letter?"

"I couldn't get a chance, and I destroyed it this morning when I learnt that she is to be married."

Chandran threw at him an angry look. He said, "Good-bye," turned round, and fled down the stairs.

The opposite house shone in the greenish brilliance of two Kitson lamps. People were coming to the house, women wearing lace-bordered *saris*, and men in well-ironed shirts and upper cloths—guests to the Wedding Notice ceremony. Chandran ran down the street, chased by the *Kalyani raga* and the doom-doom of the drummer.

Chandran had fever that night. He had a high temperature, and he raved. In about ten days, when he was well again, he insisted on being sent to Madras for a change. His father gave him fifty rupees, sent a wire to his brother at Madras to meet Chandran at the Egmore Station, and put Chandran in a train going to Madras. Chandran's mother said at the station that he must return to Malgudi very plump and fat, and without any kind of worry in his head; Father said that he could write for more money if he needed it; Seenu, who had also come to the station, asked, "Brother, do you know Messrs. Binns in Madras?"

"No," said Chandran.

"It is in Mount Road," said Seenu, and explained that it was the most magnificent sports goods firm in the country. "Please go there and ask them to send me their fat catalogue; there are a lot of cricket pictures in it. Please buy a Junior Willard bat for me. Note it down, you may forget the name, it is Binns, Junior Willard," he cried as the engine lurched, and Mother wiped her eyes, and Father stood looking after the train.

PART THREE

CHAPTER ELEVEN

§

NEXT morning, as the train steamed into the Madras Egmore Station, Chandran, watching through the window of his compartment, saw in the crowd on the platform his uncle's son. Chandran understood that the other was there to receive him, and quickly withdrew his head into the compartment. The moment the train halted, Chandran pushed his bag and hold-all into the hands of a porter, and hurried off the platform. Outside a *jutka* driver greeted him and invited him to get into his carriage. Chandran got in and said, " Drive to the hotel."

" Which hotel, master ? "

" Any hotel you like."

" Would you like the one opposite to the People's Park ? "

" Yes," said Chandran.

The *jutka* driver whipped his horse and shouted to the pedestrians to keep out of the way.

The *jutka* stopped in front of a red smoky building.

Chandran jumped out of the carriage and walked into the hotel, the *jutka* driver following him, carrying the bag and the hold-all.

A man was sitting before a table making entries in a ledger. Chandran stood before him and asked, "Have you rooms ?"

"Yes," said the man without looking up.

"My fare, sir," reminded the *jutka* driver at this point.

"How much ?" Chandran asked.

"A rupee, master. I have brought you here all the way from the station."

Chandran took out his purse and gave him a rupee, and the *jutka* driver went away gasping with astonishment. Invariably if he asked for a rupee he would be given only a quarter of it, after endless haggling and argument. Now this fare had flung out a rupee without any question. It was a good beginning for the day ; he always regretted afterwards that it hadn't occurred to him to ask for two rupees at the first shot.

The man at the table pressed a bell ; a servant appeared. The man said, "Room Three, upstairs," and gave him a key. The servant lifted the hold-all and the bag and disappeared. Chandran stood hesitating, not knowing what he was expected to do.

"The advance," said the man at the table.

"How much?" Chandran asked, wishing that the people of Madras were more human; they were so mechanical and impersonal; the porter at the station had behaved as if he were blind, deaf, and mute; now this hotel man would not even look at his guest; these fellows simply did not care what happened to you after they had received your money; the *jutka* man had departed promptly after he received the rupee, not uttering a single word. . . . Chandran had a feeling of being neglected. "How many days are you staying?" asked the man at the table. Chandran realized that he had not thought of this question; but he was afraid to say so; the other might put his hand on his neck and push him out; anything was possible in this impersonal place.

"Three days," Chandran said.

"Then a day's advance will do now," the man said, looking at Chandran for the first time.

"How much?"

"Four rupees. Upstair room four rupees a day, and downstair two-eight a day. I have sent your things to Three upstairs."

"Thank you very much," Chandran said, and gave him the advance.

His room was up a winding staircase. It was a

small room containing a chair, a table, and an iron bedstead.

Chandran sat on the bedstead and rubbed his eyes. He felt weary. He got up and stood looking out of the window: tramcars were grinding the road; motor cars, cycles, rickshaws, buses, *jutkas*, and all kinds of vehicles were going up and down in a tremendous hurry in the General Hospital Road below. Electric trains roared behind the hotel building. Chandran could not bear the noise of traffic. He returned to his bedstead and sat on it, holding his head between his hands. Somebody was humming a tune in the next room. The humming faded and then seemed to come nearer. Chandran looked up and saw a stranger, carrying a towel and a soap box, standing in the doorway. He was a dark, whiskered person. He stood for a while there, looking at Chandran unconcernedly and humming a tune.

"Not coming to bathe, friend?" he asked.

"No. I shall bathe later," replied Chandran.

"When? You won't have water in the tap after nine. Come with me. I will show you the bathroom."

From that moment the whiskered man, who announced that his name was "Kailas," took charge of Chandran. He acted as his guide and adviser in every minute detail of personal existence.

They went out together after breakfast. Chandran had absolutely no courage to oppose the other in anything. Kailas had an aggressive hospitality. He never showed the slightest toleration for any amendment or suggestion that Chandran made. Chandran was taken out and was whirled about in all sorts of tramcars and buses all day. They had tiffin in at least four hotels before the evening. Kailas paid for everything, and talked without a pause. Chandran learnt that Kailas had married two wives and loved both of them ; had years ago made plenty of money in Malaya, and had now settled down in his old village, which was about a night's journey from Madras, and that he occasionally descended on Madras in order to have a good time. "I have brought two hundred rupees with me. I shall stay here till this is spent, and then return to my village and sleep between the two wives for the next three months, and then again come here. I don't know how long it is going to last. What do you think my age is ?"

"About thirty," Chandran said, giving out the first number that came to his head.

"Ah, ah, ah ! Do you think my hair is dyed ?"

"No, no," Chandran assured him.

"In these days fellows get greying hairs before they are twenty-five. I am fifty-one. I shall be good enough for this kind of life for another twenty years at least. After that it doesn't matter what happens; I shall have lived a man's life. A man must spend forty years in making money and forty years in spending it."

By the evening Chandran felt very exhausted. To Kailas's inquiry Chandran replied that he was a student in Tanjore come out to Madras on a holiday tour.

At about five o'clock Kailas took Chandran into a building where ferns were kept in pots in the hall.

"What is this?" Chandran asked.

"Hotel Merton. I am going to have a little drink, if you don't mind."

Kailas led Chandran up a flight of stairs, and selected a table in the upstair veranda. A waiter appeared behind them.

"Have you Tenets?" Kailas asked.

"Yes, master."

"Bring a bottle and two glasses. You will have a small drink with me?" he asked, turning to Chandran.

"Beer? No, sorry. I don't drink."

"Come on, be a sport. You must keep me company."

Chandran's heart palpitated. "I never take alcohol."

"Who said that there was alcohol in beer? Less than five per cent. There is less alcohol in beer than in some of the tonics your doctors advise you to take."

The waiter came with a bottle of beer and two glasses. Kailas argued and debated till some persons sitting at other tables looked at them. Chandran was firm. In his opinion he was being asked to commit the darkest crime.

Kailas said to the waiter, "Take the beer away, boy. That young master won't drink. Get me a gin and soda. You will have lime juice?"

"Yes."

"Give that master lime juice." The waiter departed. "Why won't you have a little port or something?"

"No, no," said Chandran.

"Why not even port?"

"Excuse me. I made a vow never to touch alcohol in my life, before my mother," said Chandran. This affected Kailas profoundly. He remained solemn for a moment and said, "Then don't. Mother is a sacred object. It is a commodity whose value we don't realize as long as it is with us. One must lose it to know what a precious possession it is. If I had my mother I should have studied in a college and become a respectable person. You wouldn't find me here. After this, where do you think I am going ?"

"I don't know."

"To the house of a prostitute." He remained reflective for a moment and said with a sigh, "As long as my mother lived she said every minute 'Do this. Don't do that.' And I remained a good son to her. The moment she died I changed. It is a rare commodity, sir. Mother is a rare commodity."

The spree went on till about eight-thirty in the evening, whisky following gin, and gin following whisky. There was a steady traffic between the table and the bar. At about eight-thirty Kailas belched loudly, hiccuped thrice, looked at Chandran with red eyes, and asked if Chandran thought he was drunk; he smiled with great satisfaction when Chandran said that he did not think so.

"There are fellows," said Kailas in a very heavy voice, "who will get drunk on two pegs of brandy. I throw out a challenge to any one. Put fifteen pegs of neat whisky, neat, mind you, into this soul"—he tapped his chest—"and I will tell you my name, do any multiplication or addition, and repeat numbers from a hundred backwards."

They left the hotel. Kailas put his arm on Chandran's shoulder for support. They walked down Broadway, this strange pair. Kailas often stopped to roll his eyes foolishly and scratch his whiskers. He was discoursing on a variety of topics. He stopped suddenly in the road and asked, "Did you have anything to eat?"

"Thanks. Plenty of cakes."

"Did you drink anything?"

"Gallons of lime juice."

"Why not a little beer or something? What a selfish rascal I am!"

"No, no," said Chandran with anxiety. "I have made a vow to my mother never to touch alcohol."

"Ah!" said Kailas. He blew his nose and wiped his eyes with his kerchief. "Mother! Mother!" He remained moody for some time, and said with an air of contentment, "I know that my mother will be happy to know that I am happy." He drew in a sharp breath and moved on again resolutely, as if determined not to let his feelings overcome him.

They walked in silence to the end of the road, and Kailas said, "Why won't you call a taxi?"

" Where am I to find it ? "

Kailas gave a short, bitter laugh. " You ask me ! Go and ask that electric post. Has God made you so blind that you can't see that I can't walk owing to a vile corn on the left foot ? "

Chandran stood puzzled. He was afraid to cross the road, though the traffic was light now. Kailas appealed to him :

" Don't stand there, gaping open-mouthed at the wonders of the world, my boy. Get brisk and be helpful. Be a true friend. A friend in need is a friend indeed. Haven't you learnt it at school ? I wonder what they teach you in schools nowadays ! "

A passer-by helped Chandran to find a taxi. Kailas gave Chandran a hug when the taxi came. He got into the taxi and asked the driver, " Do you know Kokilam's house ? "

" No," replied the driver.

Kailas threw at Chandran an accusing look and said, " This is the kind of taxi you are pleased to call ! Let us get down."

" Where does she live ? " asked the taxi driver.

" Round about Mint Street."

" Ah ! " said the taxi driver, " don't I know Kokilam's house ? " He started the car, and drove it about and about for half an hour and stopped before a house in a narrow congested road. " Here it is," he said.

" Get down," said Kailas to Chandran. " How much ? "

" The meter shows fifteen rupees, eight annas," said the driver.

" Take seventeen-eight," said Kailas, and gave him the money.

The taxi drove away.

" Whose house is this ? " asked Chandran.

" My girl's house," said Kailas. He surveyed the house up and down and said doubtfully, " It looks different to-day. Never mind." He climbed the steps and asked somebody at the door, " Is this Kokilam's house ? "

" What does a name matter ? You are welcome to my poor abode, sir." It was a middle-aged woman.

" You are right," said Kailas, greatly pleased. He suddenly asked Chandran, " Did you take the taxi number ? "

" No."

" Funny man ! Do you want me to be telling you every moment what you must do ? Have you no common sense ? "

" I am sorry," said Chandran. " The taxi is over

there. I will note the number and come back." He turned round, feeling happy at this brilliant piece of strategy, and jumped down the steps of the house. Kailas muttered, "Good boy. You are a good friend in need is a friend inde-e-e-ed."

Chandran fled from Mint Street. He had escaped from Kailas. This was the first time he had been so close to a man in drink; this was the first time he had stood at the portals of a prostitute's house. He was thoroughly terrified.

After leaving Kailas several streets behind, Chandran felt exhausted and sat down on a pavement. He felt very homesick. He wondered if there was any train which would take him back to Malgudi that very night. He felt that he had left home years ago, and not on the previous evening. The thought of Malgudi was very sweet. He would walk to Lawley Extension, to his house, to his room, and sleep on his cot snugly. He lulled his mind with this vision for some time. It was not long before his searching mind put to him the question why he was wandering about the streets of a strange city, leaving his delightful heaven? The answer brought a medley of memories: piper shreiking through his pipe *Kalyani raga*, glare of Kitson lamps, astrologers, horoscopes, and unsympathetic Mother. Ah, even at this moment Malathi was probably crying into her pillow at having to marry a person she did not like. What sort of a person was he ? Would he be able to support her, and would he treat her well ? Somebody else to be her husband, and he having dreamed for weeks on the evening sands of Sarayu.

Chandran decided never to return to Malgudi. He hated the place. Everything there would remind him of Malathi—the sands on Sarayu bank, the cobbles in Market Road, Mill Street, the little shopkeeper with Malathi's eyebrows. It would be impossible for him to live again in that hell. It was a horrible town, with its preparations for Malathi's wedding. . . . Suppose even now some epidemic caught her future husband ? Such things never happened in real life.

Chandran realized that he had definitely left his home. Now what did it matter where he lived ? He was like a *sanyasi*. Why " like " ? He was a *sanyasi* ; the simplest solution. Shave the head, dye the clothes in ochre, and you were dead for aught the world cared. The only thing possible ; short of committing suicide, there was no other way out. He had done with the gamble of life. He was beaten. He could not go on living, probably for sixty years more, with people and friends and parents, with Malathi married and gone.

He got up. He wandered a little in search of his hotel, and then suddenly realized that it was quite an unnecessary search. What was he going to do after finding the hotel? Pay the bill, take the bag, and clear out somewhere? Why should a *sanyasi* carry a bag? Cast the bag and the hold-all aside, he told himself. As for payment, the hotel man had already been paid an advance, and if he wanted he could take the bag and the hold-all also into possession.

He slept that night on a pavement, rolling close to some wall. A board hung on the wall. He looked at it to make out what place it was; but the board only said "Bill Stickers Will Be Prosecuted," with its Tamil translation elaborated in meaning, "Those Who Stick Notices Will Be Handed Over To The Police." "Don't worry, I won't stick notices here," he told the wall, and lay down. The fatigue of the day brought on sleep. Bill Stickers. . . . He dreamt a number of times that while sleeping close to the wall he was mistaken for a poster, peeled off the wall by policemen, and placed under arrest.

§

Next morning he was awakened by a sweeper. Chandran sat rubbing his eyes. When his mind emerged from sleep, he resolved to get out of Madras immediately. There was no use remaining in the city any longer. It was so big and confusing that one didn't know even the way out of it. There was, moreover, the danger of being caught again by Kailas.

He found his way to the Central Station, went to a ticket counter, and asked, " When is the next train leaving ? "

" For ? "

" For—for," repeated Chandran ; " wait a minute, please." He glanced at a big railway map hanging on the wall and said, " Bezwada."

" Grand Trunk Express at seven-forty."

" One third-class, please, for Bezwada."

He got into the train. The compartment was not crowded. He suddenly felt very unhappy at having to go to Bezwada. He looked at the yellow ticket in his hand, and turned it between his fingers. . . . He was not going to be tyrannized over by that piece of yellow cardboard into taking a trip to

Bezwada. He didn't like the place, a place with the letter "z" in its name. He was not going to be driven to that place by anything. The first bell rang. He flung the ticket out of the window and jumped out of the train. He was soon out of the station.

He crossed the road, and got into a tram, and settled down comfortably in a seat. The conductor came and said, "Ticket, please."

"Where does this go?"

"Mylapore."

"One ticket, Mylapore. How much?"

For the next half-hour his problems as to where to go were set at rest. When the tram halted at the terminus he got down and walked till he saw the magnificent grey spire of Kapaleeswarar temple against the morning sky.

He entered the temple, went round the holy corridor, and prostrated before every image and sanctuary that he saw.

He saw a barber sitting on the steps of the temple tank waiting for customers. Chandran went to him and asked, "Will you shave me?"

"Yes, master." The barber was rather surprised. Young students with crops never showed any trust in him. His only customers were widows who shaved their heads completely and orthodox Brahmins who shaved their heads almost completely. Now here was a man willing to abandon his crop into his hands. Chandran said, "I will give you a lot of money if you will do me a little service."

"I can also crop well, master."

"It is not only that. You must buy a cheap loin-cloth and an upper covering for me, dye them in ochre, and bring them to me. After that you can shave my head, and take these clothes I am wearing and also the purse in my pocket." He held the purse open before him. The barber saw in it rupees and some notes, wages for six months' work in these days of safety razors and self-shaving.

"But not a word about it to any one, mind you," said Chandran.

"Are you becoming a *sanyasi* ?"

"Don't ask questions," commanded Chandran.

"Master, at your age !"

"Will you stop asking questions or shall I get into a bus and go away ? I want your help because I don't know where to get these things in this wretched place. What is your name ?"

"Ragavan."

"Ragavan, help me. You will gain my eternal gratitude. You will also profit yourself. My heart is dead, Ragavan. I have lost everybody I love in this world, Ragavan. I will be waiting for you here. Come soon."

"Master, if you don't mind, why should you not come and wait in my poor hut?"

Chandran went with him to his house, beyond a network of stifling lanes and by-lanes. It was a one-roomed house, with a small bunk attached to it, full of heat and smoke, serving as kitchen. A very tall, stout woman came out of it and asked the barber, "Why have you come back so soon?" He went near her and whispered something.

He unrolled a mat for Chandran, requested him to make himself comfortable, and went out.

Chandran's mind and spirit had become so deadened that it did not matter to him where he waited, and how long. So, though he had to spend nearly half the day alone in the barber's house, seeing nothing but the barber's oily pillow and a red rug; and a calendar picture, without month or date sheets, showing Brahma, the Creator of the Universe; and an iron-banded teakwood box, Chandran did not feel the passing of the time.

The barber returned at three o'clock in the afternoon. He brought with him two pieces of cloth dyed in ochre. He brought also a few plantains and a green coconut.

Chandran was hungry, and did not refuse the coconut and fruits. He sent the barber out again for a postcard.

When the postcard was brought, Chandran borrowed a short pencil from the barber, and wrote to his father: "Reached this place safely. I am staying with a friend I met at the station, and not with uncle. I am leaving this for . . . I won't tell you where. I am going to wander about a lot. I am quite happy and cheerful. Don't fear that I am still worried about the marriage. Not at all. I am going to wander a good deal, and so don't run to the police station if you don't hear from me for a long time. You must promise not to make a fuss. My respects to Mother. I shall be all right." He added a postscript: " Am going with some friends, old classmates, whom I met here."

CHAPTER TWELVE

§

HIS dress and appearance, the shaven pate and the ochre loin-cloth, declared him now and henceforth to be a *sanyasi*—one who had renounced the world and was untouched by its joys and sorrows.

He travelled several districts on foot. When he felt tired he stopped a passing country cart and begged for a lift. No one easily refused an obligation to a *sanyasi*. Occasionally he stopped even buses on the highway.

He never cared to know where he was going or where he was staying (except that it was not in the direction of Malgudi). For what did it matter to a *sanyasi* where he was going ? One town was very much like another : the same bazaar street, hair-cutting saloons, coffee hotels, tailors squatting before sewing-machines, grocers, Government officials, cycles, cars, and cattle. The difference was only in the name, and why should a *sanyasi* learn a name ?

When he felt hungry he tapped at the nearest

house and begged for food ; or he begged in the bazaar street for a coconut or plantain.

For the first few days his system craved for coffee, to which he was addicted since his childhood. While one part of him suffered acutely, another part derived a satisfaction in watching it writhe and in saying to it, " Go on : suffer and be miserable. You were not sent into this world to enjoy. Go on : be miserable and perish. You won't get coffee." Circumstances gradually wore this craving out.

If anybody invited him to sleep under a roof he did it ; if not, he slept in the open, or in a public rest-house, where were gathered scores like him. When he was hungry and found none to feed him, he usually dragged himself about in a weak state, and enjoyed the pain of hunger. He said to his stomach, " Rage as much as you like. Why won't you kill me ? "

His cheek bones stood out ; the dust of the highway was on him ; his limbs had become horny ; his complexion had turned from brown to a dark tan. His looks said nothing ; they did not even seem to conceal a mystery ; they looked dead. His lips rarely smiled.

He shaved once or twice and found that it was easier to allow the hair to grow as it pleased than to keep it down. His hair grew unhindered ; in course of time a very young beard and moustache encircled his mouth.

He was different from the usual *sanyasi*. Others may renounce with a spiritual motive or purpose. Renunciation may be to them a means to attain peace or may be peace itself. They are perhaps dead in time, but they do live in eternity. But Chandran's renunciation was not of that kind. It was an alternative to suicide. Suicide he would have committed but for its social stigma. Perhaps he lacked the barest physical courage that was necessary for it. He was a *sanyasi* because it pleased him to mortify his flesh. His renunciation was a revenge on society, circumstances, and perhaps, too, on destiny.

§

After about eight months of wandering he reached Koopal Village in Sainad District. It was a small village nestling at the foot of the range of mountains that connected the Eastern and the Western Ghats.

On a hot afternoon Chandran arrived in this village, and drank water in the channel that fed the paddy fields. He then went and sat in the shade of a banyan tree. He had been walking since the dawn, and he felt tired. He reclined on a stout root of the banyan and closed his eyes.

When he opened his eyes again he saw some villagers standing around him.

"May we know where our master is coming from?" somebody asked.

Chandran was tired of inventing an answer to this question. On the flash of an idea he touched his mouth and shook his head. "He is dumb."

"No, he can hear us. Can you hear us?"

Chandran shook his head in assent.

"Can you talk?"

Chandran shook his head in assent, held up his ten fingers, touched his lips, looked heavenward, and shook his head. They understood. "He is under a vow of silence of ten years or ten months or ten days."

A number of villagers stood around Chandran and gaped at him. Chandran felt rather embarrassed at being the target of the stare of a crowd. He closed his eyes. This was taken by the others for meditation.

An important man of the village came forward and asked, "Won't you come and reside in my poor abode?"

Chandran declined the offer with a gesture, and spent the night under the tree.

Next day, as the villagers passed him on their way to the fields, they saluted him with joined palms. Somebody brought a few plantains and placed them before him ; somebody else offered him milk. Chandran accepted the gifts, consumed them, and then rose to go.

Somebody asked him, " Master, where are you going ? "

With a sweep of his hands Chandran indicated a far away destination.

At this they begged him to stay. " Master, our village is so unlucky that few come this way. Bless us with your holy presence for some more days, we beg of you." Chandran shook his head, but they would not let him go. " Master, your very presence will bless our village. We rarely see holy men here. We beg of you to stay for some days more."

Chandran was touched by this request. No one had valued his presence so highly till now. He was treated with consideration everywhere, but not with so much of it as he saw here. He felt : " Poor fellows. Probably no interesting person comes this way, which is God-knows-how-far from everywhere. Why not stay if it is going to give them any pleasure. This is as good a place as another."

He went back to the banyan seat. There was great

rejoicing when he consented to stay. Men, women, and children followed him to the banyan tree.

Soon the news spread from hamlet to hamlet and village to village that a holy man under a vow of silence for ten years had arrived, and that he spent his time in rigorous meditation under a banyan tree.

Next day scores of visitors came from all the surrounding villages, and gathered under the banyan tree. Chandran sat in the correct pose of a man in meditation, cross-legged and with his eyes shut.

It never occurred to them to doubt. They were innocent and unsophisticated in most matters (excepting their factions and fights), and took an ascetic's make-up at its face value.

Late in the evening Chandran opened his eyes and saw only a few villagers standing around him. He signed to them to leave him alone. After this request was repeated twice they left him.

The night had fallen. Somebody had brought and left a lighted lantern beside him. He looked about. They had all brought gifts for him, milk and fruits and food. The sight of the gifts sent a spear through his heart. He felt a cad, a fraud, and a confidence trickster. These were gifts for a counterfeit exchange. He wished that he deserved their faith in him. The sight of the gifts made him unhappy. He ate some fruit and drank a little milk with the greatest self-deprecation.

He moved away from the gifts ; still the light shone on them. He even blew out the lantern—he did not deserve the light.

Sitting in the dark, he subjected his soul to a remorseless vivisection. From the moment he had donned the ochre cloth to the present, he had been living on charity, charity given in mistake, given on the face value of a counterfeit. He had been humbugging through life. He told himself that if he were such an ascetic he ought to do without food or perish of starvation. He ought not to feed his miserable stomach with food which he had neither earned nor, by virtue of spiritual worth, deserved.

He sought an answer to the question why he had come to this degradation. He was in no mood for self-deception, and so he found the answer in the words " Malathi " and " Love." The former had brought him to this state. He had deserted his parents, who had spent on him all their love, care, and savings. He told himself that he had surely done this to spite his parents, who probably had died of anxiety by now. This was all his return for their love and for all that they had done for him. The more he reflected on this, the greater became his anger with Malathi. It was a silly infatuation. Little sign did she show of caring for a fellow ; she couldn't say that she had no chance. She had plenty of opportunities to show that she noticed him. Where there was a will there was a way. She had only been playing with him, the devil. Women were like that, they enjoyed torturing people. And for the sake of her memory he had come to this. He railed against that memory, against love. There was no such thing ; a foolish literary notion. If people didn't read stories they wouldn't know there was such a thing as love. It was a scorching madness. There was no such thing. And driven by a non-existent thing he had become a deserter and a counterfeit.

He wondered if he ought not to stand in the village street, call everybody, and announce to them what he was. They might not believe, or they might think he had gone mad, or they might believe and feel that they were fooled and mob him and beat him to a pulp. He toyed with this vision, a punishment that he would surely deserve.

He rose. He decided to leave the village, as the most decent and practical thing that he could do. He moved out of the banyan shade.

§

Chandran walked all night, and early in the morning sighted a bus. He stopped it.

" Will you please take me in ? "

" Where are you going ? "

" In your direction."

The conductor looked at the seats and grumbled.

" I will get down anywhere you like, any time you get passengers for the full bus."

The bus was still empty, and the request came from one who wore the ochre garb, and the conductor said, " Come on."

The *sanyasi* climbed the bus and said, " I have walked all night. Put me down in a place where there is a telegraph office."

The bus conductor thought for a moment and said, " There is one at Maduram."

" How far is it from here ? "

" About ten miles, but we do not go there. We branch off about two miles from Maduram. This bus goes to Kalki."

Chandran got down from the bus at the cross-roads and walked to Maduram. It was a small town on the banks of Samari River. In the central street there was a post and telegraph office. Chandran tapped on the post office window and said to the postmaster, "I want to have a word with you. Can I come in?"

After a severe scrutiny of the visitor the postmaster said, "Yes."

Chandran went into the small post office. The postmaster looked at Chandran suspiciously. Too many English-speaking *sanyasis* were about the place now, offering to tell the future, and leaving their hosts minus a rupee or two at the end.

"You want to tell me my future, I suppose," said the postmaster.

"No, sir. I don't know any astrology."

"Too many *sanyasis* come here nowadays. We simply can't afford to pay for all the astrology that is available."

"I wish I had at least that to give in exchange," said Chandran, and then opened his heart to the postmaster. He gave a clear account of his life and troubles.

After hearing his story the postmaster agreed to lend him a rupee and eight annas for sending a telegram to his father for money.

Chandran expressed a desire for a shave and a change of clothing. The postmaster sent for a barber and gave Chandran an old shirt and a white *dhoti*.

Chandran requested the barber to pay special attention to his head, and to use the scissors carefully there. He also requested the barber to shave his face thrice over.

After that he went in for a bath, and came out of the bathroom feeling resurrected. He was dressed in the postmaster's *dhoti* and shirt. He had in his hand his *sanyasi* robes in a bundle. After inviting the postmaster to witness the sight, he flung the bundle over the wall into the adjoining lane.

He asked for a little hair oil and a comb. He rubbed the oil on his head and tried to comb his hair before a mirror.

The feel of a shirt on his body and of a smooth chin, after months of shirtless and prickly existence, gave him an ecstatic sensation.

At about four in the afternoon a message arrived endowing Chandran with fifty rupees, though he had wired for only twenty-five.

The mail train towards Madras passed Maduram station at one o'clock at night. Chandran bought a ticket for Malgudi, changed trains at two junctions, and finally got down at Malgudi station in the morning two days later.

PART FOUR

CHAPTER THIRTEEN

§

HIS parents were amazed to see him so transformed.

" I should have come to the station, Chandar," said his father, " but I was not sure when you were coming."

Mother said, " You are looking like a corpse. How your bones stick out! What sunken cheeks! What were you at all these days?"

Seenu said, " What about the cricket bat? Where is your coat? Your shirt is a bit loose. You have also spoilt your crop. It is very short. Where is your bag?"

Father and Mother looked very careworn.

Mother asked, " Why couldn't you write to us at least a card?"

" I did," said Chandran.

" Only one. You should have written to us at least once after that."

Father asked, " Did you travel much? What were the places you visited?"

"Lots of places. Rolled about a great deal," said Chandran, and stopped at that. His father could never get more than that from him.

"Why didn't you go to your uncle's?"

"I didn't fancy him," said Chandran. "Were you all very greatly worried about me?"

"Your mother was. She thought that something terrible had happened to you. Every morning she troubled me to go and inform the police." He turned to his wife and added, "Have I not been telling you that you were merely imagining things?"

"Ah," she said, "as if you weren't anxious! How many times did you say that an announcement must be made in the papers?"

Father looked abashed.

Chandran asked, "I hope you haven't told the police or advertised in the papers?"

"No, no," said Father. "But I should certainly have done something if I hadn't heard from you for some weeks more. It was only your mother who was very, very worried."

"As if you weren't," Mother retorted. "Why did you go thrice to Madras, and then to Trichinopoly, and write to all sorts of people?"

Seenu said, "Father and Mother were worried about you, brother. Nobody would talk to me in this house. They were all very ill-tempered and morose all these months. I didn't like our house, brother. No one to talk to in the house except the cook. You ought to have written to us at least once or twice. I hoped that you would go to Binns and bring at least their catalogue."

Chandran went to his room and there found everything just as he had left it. The books that had been kept on the table were there ; the cot in the same position, the bookshelf in the same old place, his old grey coat on the same hook on the coat stand ; the table near the window with even the writing-pad in the same position. There was not a speck of dust on anything, nor a single spider's web. In fact the room and all the objects in it were tidier than they had ever been. The sight of things spick and span excited him. Everything excited him now. He ran to his mother and asked, panting, " Mother, how is it everything is so neat in my room ? "

Father replied, " She swept and cleaned it with great care every day."

" Why did you take so much trouble, Mother ? "

She became red and was embarrassed. " What better business did I have ? "

" How did you manage to keep Seenu out of my room, Mother ? "

"Mother used to lock up the room, and never left it open even for an hour," Seenu replied.

Chandran suddenly asked, "What has happened to Ramu? Did anybody hear from him?"

"No."

"No letters from him for me?"

"None," his mother replied.

"Where are his people? Are they not in the next house?"

"His father was transferred to some Telegu district, and they have cleared out of this place, bag and baggage."

Chandran realized that this was the last he would hear of Ramu. Ramu was dead as far as Chandran was concerned. Ramu was never in the habit of writing. Except one card he had not written for nearly two years now. His people till now were in the next house, and there was some hope of hearing about him. Now that too was gone. Chandran reflected gloomily, "I and he are parted now. He won't bother about me any more. Very frivolous minded. Won't bother about a thing that is out of sight."

Mother said, "They came here to take leave of us, and they said that Ramu had found an appointment at seventy-five rupees a month in the Bombay railways."

Chandran felt very hurt on hearing this. Here was a person who didn't care to communicate to a friend such happy news as the securing of a job. That was like Ramu. Friendship was another illusion like Love, though it did not reach the same mad heights. People pretended that they were friends, when the fact was they were brought together by force of circumstances. The classroom or the club or the office created friendships. When the circumstances changed the relations, too, snapped. What did Ramu care for him now, after all the rambles on the river, cigarettes, cinema, and confidences ? Friendship—what meaningless expressions had come into use !

" What is the matter, Chandra, you are suddenly moody ? " asked Chandran's father.

" Nothing, nothing," said Chandran. " I was only thinking of something. Father, have you any idea where your old college friends are now ? "

Father tried to recollect. He gave up the attempt. " I don't know. If I look at the old college group photo I may be able to tell you something." He turned to his wife and asked, " Where is that group photo ? "

" How should I know ? " she replied.

Seenu said, " I don't know if it is the one you want. I found a large group photo in the junk room, and I have hung it over my table, but the glass is broken."

Chandran said, "I don't mean the whole class. Just some particular friends you had in the college."

"For the four years I spent in the Christian College I had about three or four intimate friends. We were room-mates and neighbours in the hostel. We were always together. . . . Sivaraman, he entered the Imperial Service and was in Bihar for some time. It is over thirty years since we wrote to each other. I recently saw in the papers that he retired as Chief something or other in the Railway Board. Gopal Menon, he was in the Civil Service. He died some time ago of heart failure. This, too, I saw only in the papers, and then wrote a condolence letter to his wife. The other, we used to call him Kutti, his full name was something or other. I don't know where he is now. The only old friend who is still in this town is Madhava Rao."

"You mean the old man who lives near the college?"

"No, that is another person. I am referring to K. T. Madhava Rao, the retired Postal Superintendent. He and I were very intimate friends."

"Do you meet often now?"

"Once in a way. He doesn't come to the club.

Now that you ask me, I remember I went to his house about four years ago, when he was laid up with blood pressure."

" And you used to spend all your time together in the college ? "

" Yes, yes. But you see. . . . We can't afford to be always together, you know. Each of us has to go his own way."

To Chandran it was a depressing revelation. Well, probably ages hence he would be saying to his grandson, "I had a friend called Ramu. It is fifty years since we have written to each other. I don't know if he is still living." His father at least had a group photo in the junk room ; he hadn't even that—he had simply forgotten to buy his class group. " . . . this too I saw only in the papers. . . ." The callousness of Time !

He stepped down into the garden. He found the garden paths overgrown with grass, and plants in various stages of decay. Thick weeds had sprung up everywhere, and were choking a few cretons and roses that were still struggling for life. He had never seen the garden in this state. Ever since he could remember his father had worked morning and evening in the garden. Now what had happened to the gardener ? What had happened to Father ?

He went in and asked, " What has happened to the plants ? "

Father looked awkward and said, " I don't know. . . ."

" What, have you not been gardening ? "

" I couldn't attend to the plants," he said.

" What were you busy with, then ? "

" I don't know what account to give of myself."

Mother said mischievously, " He was busy searching for a missing son."

" But I wrote to you, Father, that you wouldn't hear from me for a long time and not to worry."

" Oh, yes, you did. It wasn't that. Your mother is only joking. Don't take her seriously."

Chandran went to Mohan's hotel in the evening. Before starting, he said to his mother, " I may not come back to-night. I shall sleep in Mohan's hotel."

§

As he approached Mohan's hotel he could not help recollecting with a grim detachment the state of mind he was in the last time he was here. The detachment was forced, his heart beat fast as he came in front of the Modern Indian Lodge. Suppose she was standing at that very moment at the entrance of the opposite house ? Before slipping into the hotel, in spite of his resolve, he turned his head once; but there was no one at the entrance. As he climbed the staircase he reproached himself severely for this. Still a prey to illusions! Was he making for another bout of asceticism and wandering ?

He stopped at the landing and found Room 14 locked. On the door some other name was scrawled in pencil. Chandran descended the stairs and asked the manager if Mohan was still in the hotel.

"Room 14," said the manager.

"But it is locked. Some other name on the door."

"That is the old Fourteen. The new Fourteen is on the topmost floor."

Chandran went up and found Mohan in a newly-built small room at the topmost part of the building. It was airy and bright, a thorough contrast to the wooden-partitioned cell on the landing. There were a table and a chair; a few pictures on the wall. Everything tidy.

Mohan was speechless for five minutes, and then he opened his mouth and let out a volley of questions: "What did you do with yourself ? Where were you ? Why. . . ."

"This is really a splendid room!" Chandran said. "How did you manage to leave the old one ?"

"I am prosperous now, you see," Mohan said happily. "Tell me about yourself."

"Mine is a long story. It is like *Ramayanam*. You will hear it presently. Tell me how you are prospering."

"Quite well, as I told you. The *Daily Messenger* now sells a total of thirty thousand copies a day. They pay me now five rupees a column, and don't cut much because they want to establish a good circulation in these districts. New company running it now. They are very regular in payment. I am making nearly twenty columns a month. Besides this, they publish my poems once a week in their magazine page, and pay me four annas a line." Mohan looked very healthy and cheerful.

"This is great news," said Chandran. "I am glad you have left that old cell."

"I am paying five rupees more for this room. I insisted on this room being called Fourteen. It is a lucky number. So this is known as the New Fourteen, and the other as the Old Fourteen. This room was built very recently. The hotel proprietor is very prosperous now ; he has purchased this building, and has added many rooms. The poor fellow was down in luck for a number of years ; but now lots of guests come here, and he is doing very well. I thought of shifting to another hotel, but hadn't the heart to do it. The old man and I have been friends since our bad days. In those days sometimes he would not have a measure of rice in the whole hotel; and I have several times borrowed a rupee or two and given it to him for running the hotel."

After attempting to smother the question a dozen times Chandran asked, "Are they still in the opposite house?"

Mohan smiled a little and paused before answering, "Soon after the marriage they left that house. I don't know where they are now."

"Who is living in the house now?"

"Some *marwari*, a moneylender, has acquired it."

Everywhere there seemed to be change. Change, change, everywhere. Chandran hated it. "Have I been away for only eight months or eighteen years?" Chandran asked himself. "Mohan, let us go and spend the whole evening and night on Sarayu bank. I have a lot of things to tell you. I want you. Let us eat something at an hotel and go to the river."

Mohan demurred. His presence was urgently needed at an Adjourned Meeting of the Municipality.

Chandran turned a deaf ear to the call of duty, and insisted on seducing Mohan away from the meeting.

Mohan yielded, saying, "I shall take it from the *Gazette* man to-morrow. I have got to report it to my paper."

They went to a coffee hotel, and then to the river bank. Long after the babble of the crowd on the sands had died, and darkness had fallen on the earth, Chandran's voice was heard, in tune with the rumble of the flowing river, narrating to Mohan his wanderings. He then explained his new philosophy, which followed the devastating discovery that Love and Friendship were the veriest illusions. He explained that people married because their sexual appetite had to be satisfied and there must be somebody to manage the house. There was nothing deeper than that in any man and woman relationship.

The Taluk Office gong sounded eleven at night when Chandran said, "Remember, I have not told any one that I was a *sanyasi* for eight months. You must keep it all to yourself. I don't want any one to talk about me."

They rose and walked back to the hotel through the silent streets.

CHAPTER FOURTEEN

§

CHANDRAN settled down to a life of quiet and sobriety. He felt that his greatest striving ought to be for a life freed from distracting illusions and hysterics.

He tended the garden a great deal now. Every morning he spent over two hours in the garden. He divided his time between plants and books. In the evening he took his bicycle (a second-hand one that he had bought recently) and went out for long rides on the Trunk Road. Late in the evening he went to Mohan's hotel.

This kind of life was conducive to quiet and, possibly, sobriety. With an iron will he chased away distracting illusions, and conscientiously avoided hysterics, with the care of one walking on a tight-rope. He decided not to give his mind a moment of freedom. All the mischief started there. Whatever he did, he did it with a desperate concentration now. If he dug the garden, the mind was allowed to play about only the soil and the pick. If he read a book, he tried to make the print a complete drug for the mind. The training of the mind was done feverishly and unsparingly.

There were still sights and sounds and hours which breathed, through some association or other, memories of Malathi. But he avoided them. He rarely went to the river before sundown ; and never to the old spot. He was glad that the house opposite to the Modern Indian Lodge was now occupied by a moneylender. The sound of pipe music, especially when *Kalyani raga* was played on it, disturbed his equanimity ; when going to Mohan's hotel, he carefully avoided the route that took him by the Shiva temple, where there was pipe music every evening. He never looked at the shop in Market Road for fear of encountering the eyebrows of the boy in the shop. Even then something or other was sure to remind him of Malathi and trouble him. At such moments he fumigated his mind with reflections : this is a mischievous disturbance ; this is false ; these thoughts of Malathi are unreal because Love is only a brain affection ; it led me to beg and cheat ; to desert my parents ; it is responsible for my mother's extra wrinkles and grey hairs, for my father's neglect of the garden ;

and a poor postmaster is a shirt and a *dhoti* less on account of my love.

However, there was another matter that troubled him, which could not be forced off the mind. It was the question of occupation. He often told himself that he was making arrangements to go to England in the coming year, and that he ought to come back from there with some distinction, and then search for employment. Sometimes this quietened his mind, sometimes not. He was getting on for twenty-four. It was nearly two years since he left college, and he was still leeching on his father. He was so much bothered by this thought one day that he went to his father in the garden and asked, " Why should I not apply for a Government post ? "

Father looked up from the bed of annuals that he was digging. " Why do you want to do it ? "

Chandran mumbled something.

Father understood that something was troubling him and said, " Well, there is no hurry."

" But I have wasted a lot of time already, Father. It is nearly two years since I became a graduate, and I have neither studied further nor done anything else."

" It is no waste," Father said. " You have been

reading and getting to know people and life and so on. Don't worry. Time enough to apply for jobs after you return from England. It will be really worth while, you see. There is no use in getting a bare forty or fifty as a clerk, though even that would be difficult to secure in these days."

"But I am nearly twenty-four, Father, not a baby. There are fellows who support a family at my age."

"Well, you too could have done it if it was necessary. You could have finished your college before you were twenty if I hadn't put you to school late, and if you hadn't been held up by typhoid for a year."

Chandran admired his father for admitting as causes of wasted time late schooling and typhoid, and leaving out of account the vagrant eight months, but for which he would have been in England already. Chandran comforted himself by saying that he would compensate for all this by doing something really great in England and getting into some really high post in the Education service. His father was constantly writing to his brother at Madras for a lot of preliminary information connected with Chandran's trip to England. These letters gave Chandran a feeling of progress towards an earning life. But there were times when he doubted this too. He wondered if he really ought to put his father to that expense. He wondered if his comfort from the thought of going to England soon was not another illusion, and if it would not be super-parasitic of him. He could not decide the issue himself. He consulted Mohan. Mohan asked why, if he felt so, he should not do something else. Chandran asked what, and Mohan explained, " Why not the Chief Agency of our paper ? They are not satisfied with the present agent, and have given him notice. They have advertised for an agent in this and in a few other districts."

" What is it likely to bring ? "

" It all depends. If you canvas a large circulation, you will make a lot of money."

Chandran was sceptical. " Where am I to go and canvas ? "

" That is what an agent gets his income for. In six months the daily circulation of the *Messenger* has gone up to thirty thousand, quite a good figure, and it circulates all over the Presidency. It ought to find a sale in this place also. But for the agent the circulation would not have gone above a bare twenty-five. All the same they are publishing my news because they hope that it will ultimately pull up the circulation."

Chandran was not quite convinced that it was a very useful line to take.

Next day Mohan came out with further information. "I saw the present agent. He gets a quarter of an anna per paper sold." Mohan wrote to the office for information, and in due course, when it arrived, passed it on to Chandran. After some more talk and thought, Chandran became quite enthusiastic. He asked his father, "Will you be disappointed if I don't go to England?"

"What is the matter? I have already written for official information."

"'I feel that going to England will only mean a lot of expense."

"You need not worry about that."

"Getting a distinction and coming back and securing a suitable appointment, all these seem to be a gamble."

Father was silent. He felt nervous when Chandran came and proposed anything. But Chandran went on developing exquisitely the theme of the *Messenger* agency. He saw in it a beautiful vision of an independent life full of profit and leisure. He quoted facts and figures. A quarter of an anna per day per paper sold. With a miserly circulation of 1,000 for the whole district, he would be making 250 annas a day. He would get at that rate about 480 rupees a month, which one couldn't dream of getting in the Government service even after fifteen years of slavery. And there was always the possibility of expanding the business. He gave the area of Malgudi, its population, out of which the English-knowing persons were at least 10,000; out of which number at least 5,000 would be able to spend an anna a day on a newspaper; and it was these who were going to support the *Daily Messenger*.

"For the agency we must give a security of 2,000 rupees, for which they later pay interest. Somebody has written from the office that a number of people have already applied and that there is a keen fight for the agency. They are selecting the agent only on the first. It is a good chance, Father. I think it is better than going to England."

Father listened in silence.

Mother, who was twisting small cotton bits into wicks for the lamps in God's room, said, "I think so. Why should he go to England?"

Father replied that the question could not be so easily settled. He was very ignorant of the newspaper business. He wrote a letter to his brother in Madras for enlightenment on the subject. That evening, in the club, he took aside Nanjundiah, a barrister of the town, a public figure, and his particular friend, and asked him, "Do you read the *Daily Messenger*?"

"Yes."

"What sort of a paper is it? I saw a copy, but I should like to have your opinion."

"I don't subscribe for it but get it from a neighbour. It is quite a good paper, non-party and independent."

"You see," said Chandran's father, "my son wants to take up the agency, giving a security of 2,000 rupees. I have absolutely no idea what it is all about, but he seems to think that it will be a good investment."

"What about his going to England?"

"Seems to be more keen on this. I don't know, that boy gets a new notion every day; but I don't like to stand in his way if it is really a sound proposition."

He said to Chandran that night: "I spoke to Nanjundiah about the paper. He thinks well of it, but doesn't know anything else. However, he has promised to find out and tell me."

Chandran said, "We can't be wasting time over all these inquiries. There is a rush for the agency. We must look sharp."

After Chandran had gone to his room, his mother said, " Why are you tormenting the boy ? " Father did not vouchsafe an answer but merely rustled his paper. She repeated the question, and he said, " Why don't you leave it to me ? "

" If the boy wishes to stay here, why won't you let him stay ? What is the use of sending him to England ? Waste of a lot of money. What do our boys, who go to England, specially achieve ? They only learn to smoke cigarettes, drink wine, and dance with white girls."

" It is my hope that our boy will do something more than that."

" If there is as much money in the paper as he says, why shouldn't he do that work ? "

" If there is ; that is what I must know before I let him do it. I can't very well give him a cheque for 2,000 rupees and ask him to invest it, without knowing something about the persons that are running the paper, how long it will last, and other things. There is hardly any sense in letting him in for work which may not last even a year ! I have written to my brother. Let me see what he writes."

" You have to write to your brother about everything," she said, rising to go in. " Only I don't want you to drive the boy to desperation."

Father looked after her for a long time, shifted in his easy-chair a little, and rustled the paper.

Chandran said to himself: "I have no business to hustle and harass my father. He has every right to wait and delay. If I am destined to get the agency, I shall get it; if not, I shall not get it for all the hustling."

There was a delay of four or five days before a reply arrived from his uncle. Till then Father went about his business without mentioning the paper, and Chandran too conducted himself as if there was no such thing as the *Daily Messenger*. But every morning he went out at about nine o'clock, met the Lawley Extension postman on the way and asked if there was any letter for Father. At last, one morning, the postman carried a letter in his hand for Father. It bore the Madras postmark. At other times Chandran would have snatched the letter from the postman, taken it to his father, and demanded to be told of its contents. But now he curbed that impulse, asked the postman to carry the letter himself, went to the Town Reading-room, and returned home at midday. He did not go before Father at all, but confined his movements between the kitchen and the dining-hall, till Father himself called Chandran and gave him the letter. Chandran opened the letter and read: "... There is an influential directorate at the head of the paper. J. W. Prabhu, Sir N. M. Rao, and others are on it. An agency would really be worth while, but would not be easy to secure. If you send Chandran over here immediately I shall see if anything can be done through a friend of mine who knows the Managing Director. . . ."

Chandran read the letter twice, gave it back to his father, and asked as casually as possible, "What do you think of it?"

"You can go to Madras to-day. I shall send a wire to your uncle."

"All right."

He went to his mother and said, "I am starting for Madras to-day."

She asked anxiously, "When will you be back?"

"In two or three days, as soon as my work is finished."

"Are you sure?"

"Oh, don't worry, Mother. I shall positively come back."

He immediately started packing his trunk. As he sat in his room, with all his clothes lying scattered about, his father frequently came in with something or other for Chandran in hand. He brought half a dozen kerchiefs.

"You may want these in Madras." He came next with a pair of new *dhoties*. "I have a lot more in the chest of drawers." He then brought a woollen scarf and requested Chandran to hand it over to his brother in Madras. Mother came in and asked if Chandran would like to carry anything to eat on the way. She then expressed a desire to send a small basket of vegetables to her sister-in-law. Chandran said that he would not take it with him. But she argued that she wasn't asking him to carry the load on his head. He threatened that if he were given any basket he would throw it out of the train.

At five o'clock he had finished his dinner and was ready to start. His steel trunk and a roll of bedding were brought to the hall. Mother added a small basket to Chandran's luggage. Chandran protested at the sight of the basket. Mother lifted the basket and said, "See, it is very light; contains only some vegetables for your aunt. You mustn't go with bare hands."

His father, mother, and Seenu saw Chandran off at the station. Seenu said, "Don't stay away long. Don't forget Binns this time."

§

Next morning as the train steamed into the Madras Egmore station Chandran, peeping out of the window, saw his uncle on the platform.

His uncle was about forty years old, a cheerful plump man with a greying crop, and wearing thick-rimmed spectacles. He was a business man and a general broker, doing a lot of work, and knowing all possible persons in the city.

As Chandran got down from the train, his uncle said, " I came here myself in order that you might not slip away this time."

Chandran blushed and said, " Father has sent you a scarf."

" So after all he has the strength to part with it. Is it the same or a different one ? "

" Deep blue wool."

" It is the same. He wouldn't give it to me for years."

A porter carried the things to a car outside. Chandran sat with his uncle in the front seat.

" How do you like this car ? " his uncle asked.

" It is quite good."

" I bought it recently, giving away my old Essex in exchange."

" Oh," said Chandran. He felt quite happy that his uncle was speaking to him like an equal, and was not teasing him as he used to do before. Chandran had always avoided his uncle if he could, but now he found him quite tolerable.

His uncle asked why Chandran had dropped the idea of going to England. He chatted incessantly as he drove along, cutting across tramcars, hooting behind pedestrians, and taking turns recklessly.

He lived in a bungalow in the Luz Church Road. Chandran's aunt and cousins (one of his own age, a youngster, and a girl) were standing on the veranda to receive Chandran.

" Ah, how tall Chandra has grown ! " said his aunt ; and Chandran felt very tall and proud.

" Mother has sent a basket of vegetables for you, Aunt," he said, and surveyed his cousins. The one of his own age smiled and said, " I came to the station last time."

" Oh," said Chandran, and blushed. When were people going to forget his last trip ?

" Raju, take Chandra's things to your room, and then show him the bathroom," Uncle said to this cousin.

His cousin took him to his room. Chandran removed his coat, and Raju said again, " I came to the station last time, and searched for you on the platform."

Chandran paid no attention, but opened his trunk, took out a towel and soap, and sternly said, " Show me the bathroom."

The boy seemed to be a half-wit, incapable of talking of any other subject.

When Chandran was combing his hair, his aunt brought in a very small child with curly hair and large eyes, and said, "Have you seen this girl? She is just up from bed. She simply wouldn't stay in it, but wanted to be taken to you immediately."

Chandran tapped its cheeks with his fingers. " What is her name ? "

" Kamala," replied his aunt.

" Ah, Kamal. What, Kamala ? " Chandran asked, staring at the child, and raising his hand once again to tap its cheeks. The child looked at him fixedly for a moment and began to cry. Chandran stood still, not knowing what he was expected to do. Aunt took away the child, saying, " She can't stand new faces. She will be all right when she gets to know you a little more."

At eleven o'clock, after food, his uncle took him out in the car. The car stopped before a four-storeyed building in Linga Chetty Street.

He followed his uncle up three flights of stairs, past a corridor and a glass door, into an office. Before a table littered with files a man was sitting.

His uncle said, " Good-morning, Murugesam."

" Hallo, hallo, come in," said the man at the table, pushing aside a file that he was reading.

Uncle said, " This is my nephew whom I spoke to you about. This is Mr. S. T. Murugesam, General Manager of Engladia Limited."

Chandran stretched his hand across the table and said, " I am glad to meet you, sir."

" Take a chair," said Murugesam.

Uncle and Murugesam talked for a while, and then Uncle got up. " I shall have to be going now. Some railway people are coming to my office at twelve. So you will take this boy and fix him up ? "

" I will do my best."

" That is not enough," said Uncle. " You have got to fix him up. He is a graduate, son of a big Government pensioner ; he will give any security you want. You must fix him up. He has even cancelled his trip to England for the sake of this paper. . . . You can keep him here. I shall pick him up on my way back." He went out.

Murugesam looked at the time and said, " We

shall go out at two o'clock. I hope you won't mind half an hour's wait."

"Not at all. You can take your own time, sir," said Chandran, and leant back in his chair. Murugesam signed a heap of papers, pushed them away, gripped the telephone on the table, and said into it, "Shipping," and waited for a moment and said, "Inform Damodars that we can't load *Waterway* before Thursday midnight. Thursday midnight. Bags are still arriving. She is not sailing before Saturday evening. . . . Right. Thank you."

Chandran watched him, fascinated. For the first time he was witnessing a business man at work. Chandran felt a great admiration for Murugesam, a slight man, keeping in his hands the strings of mighty activities; probably ships were waiting to sail at a word from him. How did he pick up so much business knowledge? What did he earn? Ten thousand? What did he do with so much money? When would he find time to spend the money and enjoy life with so many demands on his attention? The telephone bell rang. Murugesam took it up and said, "That is right. Tell them they will get the notice in due course. Thank you," and put down the receiver. An assistant brought in some letters and put them before him, Murugesam wrote something on them, gave them back to the assistant, and said, "I am going out, and shall not be back for about half an hour. If there are any urgent calls, you can ring me up at the *Daily Messenger*."

"Yes, sir."

"But remember, don't send any one there. Only very urgent calls." He rose and picked up his fur cap. Chandran was impressed with the other's simplicity of dress. He was wearing only a *dhoti*, a long silk coat, and a black fur cap.

He led Chandran out of the building, and got into a sedan. They drove in the car for about a quarter of an hour through whirling traffic, and got down before a new, white building in Mount Road, before which stood in huge letters the sign "*Daily Messenger*." They went up in a lift, through several halls filled with tables and men bent in work, past shining counters and twisting passages. Murugesam pushed a red-curtained door. A man was sitting at a table littered with files. "Hallo, Murugesam," he said. He was a pink, bald man, wearing rimless glasses. A fan was whirring over his head.

"I have brought this young man to see you," Murugesam said.

The bald man looked at Chandran coldly, and said

to Murugesam, "You were not at the club yesterday."

"I couldn't come. Had to go to the wharf."

A servant brought in a visiting card. The bald man looked at it critically and said, "No more interviews to-day. To-morrow at one-thirty."

Murugesam went over to the other side of the table and spoke in whispers to the bald man. Murugesam almost sat on the arm of the bald man's revolving chair. Chandran was not asked to sit, and so he stood, uncertainly, looking at the walls, with his arms locked behind him. The bald man suddenly looked at Chandran and asked, "Your father is?"

"H. C. Venkatachala Iyer."

"He was?"

"A District Judge."

"I see," said the bald man. He turned to Murugesam and said, "I have no idea what they are doing in regard to the agencies. I must ask Sankaran. I will let you know afterwards."

Murugesam made some deprecating noises and said, "That won't do. Call up Sankaran and tell him what to do. Surely you can dictate." He left the arm of the chair and went to another chair, saying, "He is a graduate, comes from a big family, prepared to give any security. He has cancelled his tour to England for the sake of your paper."

"Why did you want to go to England?" asked the bald man, turning to Chandran.

"Wanted to get a doctorate."

"At?"

"The London University."

"In?"

"Economics or Politics," said Chandran, choosing his subject for the first time.

"Why do you want to work for our paper?"

"Because I like it, sir."

"Which? The paper or the agency?"

"Both," said Chandran.

"Are you confident of sending up the circulation if you are given a district?"

"Yes, sir."

"By how much?"

Chandran quoted 5,000, and explained the figures with reference to the area of Malgudi, its literate population, and the number of people who could spend an anna a day.

"That is a fair offer," said Murugesam.

The bald man said with a dry smile, "It is good to be optimistic."

"Optimistic or not, you must give him a fair trial," said Murugesam.

The bald man said, "The trouble is that I don't usually interfere in these details. The managers concerned look to it. I have no idea what they are doing."

"Well, well, well," said Murugesam impatiently. "There is no harm in it. You can break the rule occasionally and dictate. Just for my sake. I have to go back to the office. Hurry up. Send for Sankaran." Murugesam pressed a bell. A servant came. Murugesam said, "Tell Mr. Sankaran to come up."

A man with a scowling face came in, nodded, went straight to a chair, sat down, and leaned forward.

The bald man asked, "Have you any vacancies in the Southern Districts?"

"For correspondents? No."

"I mean agencies."

"Yes, a few where we want to change the present agents."

"Yours is Malgudi, is it not?" asked the bald man, turning to Chandran.

"Yes, sir."

"I think that is one of the places," said Sankaran.

The bald man said, " Please give me some details of the place."

Sankaran pressed a bell, scribbled something on a bit of paper, and gave it to the servant. " Take it to Sastri."

The servant went out and returned in a few minutes followed by an old man, who was carrying a register with him. He placed the register on the table before Sankaran, opened a page, and stood away respectfully.

Murugesam said at this point, " Sit down, Mr. Chandran."

" Yes, yes, why are you standing ? " asked the bald man.

Chandran sat in a chair and looked at the bald man, Sankaran, the turban-wearing Sastri, and Murugesam, and thought : " My life is in these fellows' hands ! Absolute strangers. Decision of my fate in their hands, absolutely ! Why is it so ? "

Sankaran said, looking at the register, " Here are the facts, sir. Malgudi Agency : The present man has been there since the old régime. The top circulation 35 till two years ago ; since then steady at 25 ! Eleven applications for the agency up to date ; one from the old agent himself promising to turn over a new leaf. Potential circulation in the district, 7,000."

"Thank you," said the bald man. "When are you settling it?"

"I want to wait till the first."

"Why should there be any delay? If you have no particular objection, give the agency to this gentleman. He promises to give the security immediately and work for the paper."

Sankaran looked at Chandran and said to the bald man, "Some more applications may be coming in, sir."

"File them."

"Very well, sir," said Sankaran, and rose. "Come with me," he said to Chandran.

Sankaran took Chandran into a hall, where a number of persons were seated at tables, from the edges of which galley proofs streamed down to the floor. They went to the farthest end of the hall and sat down. Sankaran began a short speech on the *Daily Messenger*: "The *Daily Messenger* is not the old paper that it was a year or two ago. The circulation has gone up from 8,000 to 30,000 in less than a year. That is due both to the circulation and the editorial departments. They have both work to do, just as you need both legs for walking." He spoke over the din of the office and of the press below for half an hour, winding up with the threat that if Chandran did not show real progress within six months from the date of appointment, the agency would be immediately transferred to another.

CHAPTER FIFTEEN

§

CHANDRAN returned to Malgudi and plunged himself in work. He took a small room in Market Road for a rent of seven rupees a month, and hung on the doorway an immense sign : " *THE DAILY MESSENGER* (Local Offices)." He furnished his office with a table, a chair and a long bench.

He sat in his office from eleven till five, preparing a list of possible subscribers in the town. At the lowest estimate there were five hundred. After enlisting them, he would go out into the district and enlist another five hundred ; and for six months he would be quite content to stay at a thousand.

He took out a sheet of paper and noted on it the procedure to be followed in canvassing. He often bit the pen and looked at the traffic in Market Road, steeped in thought. After four days of intense thinking and watching of traffic, he was able to sketch out a complete plan of attack. He wrote :

" Bulletin ; Specimen ; Interview ; Advance." He would first send his bulletin to the persons on his list, then supply free specimen copies for two days, then go and see them in person, and finally take a month's subscription in advance.

Next he planned the Bulletin. It approached a client in four stages : Information ; Illumination ; Appeal ; and Force.

Bulletin One said : " Mr. H. V. Chandran, B.A., requests the pleasure of your company with family and friends at C–96 Market Road, where he has just opened the local offices of the *Daily Messenger* of Madras." Bulletin Two said : " Five reasons why you should immediately subscribe to the *Daily Messenger* : Its daily circulation is 30,000 in the Presidency, and 30,000 persons cannot be making a mistake every day. It is auspicious to wake to the thud of a paper dropped on the floor ; and we are prepared to provide you with this auspicious start every morning by bringing the *D. M.* to your house and pushing it in through your front window. It has at its command all the news services in the world, so that you will find in it a Municipal Council resolution in Malgudi as well as a political assassination in Iceland, reported accurately and quickly. The mark of culture is wide information ; and the *D. M.*

will give you politics, economics, sports, literature; and its magazine supplement covers all the other branches of human knowledge. Even in mere bulk you will be getting your anna's worth; if you find the contents uninteresting you can sell away your copy to the grocer at a rupee per *maund*." Bulletin Three said: "As a son of the Motherland it is your duty to subscribe to the *D. M.* With every anna that you pay, you support the anæmic child, Indian Industry. You must contribute your mite for the economic and political salvation of our country." Bulletin Four merely stated: "To the hesitant. It is never too late. Come at once to C–96 Market Road and take your paper, or shall we send it to your house? Never postpone to a to-morrow what you can do to-day."

He gave these for printing to the Truth Printing Works, which was situated in another room like his, four doors off. The Truth Works consisted of a treadle, a typeboard, and a compositor, besides the proprietor.

The printer delivered the bulletins in about a week. Chandran put them in envelopes and addressed them according to the list he had prepared. He had now in his service three small boys for distributing the paper, and he had purchased for them three cheap cycles. He divided the town into three sections and allotted each of them a section, and gave them the envelopes for distribution. He sent the bulletins out in their order, one on each day.

After that he engaged a small party of brass band and street boys, and sent them through the principal streets of the town in a noisy procession, in which huge placards, shrieking out the virtues of the *Daily Messenger*, were carried.

He then distributed a hundred copies of the *Messenger* every day as specimens to the persons to whom he had sent the bulletins.

After all this preparation, he set out every morning on his cycle, neatly shaved and groomed, and dressed in an impeccable check suit, and interviewed his prospects. He took the town ward by ward. He calculated that if he worked from eight in the morning till eight in the evening he would be able to see about thirty-six prospects a day, giving about twenty minutes to each prospect.

He sent his card into every house and said as soon as his prospect appeared, " Good-morning, sir. How do you like our paper ? " Soon he became an adept salesman, and in ten minutes could classify and label the person before him. He now realized that humanity fell into four types : (1) Persons who cared for the latest news and could afford an anna a day. (2) Persons who were satisfied with stale news in old papers which could be borrowed from neighbours. (3) Persons who read newspapers in reading rooms. (4) Persons who could be coerced by repeated visits.

Chandran talked a great deal to 1 and 4, and never wasted more than a few seconds on 2 and 3.

He visited club secretaries, reading-room secretaries, headmasters of schools, lawyers, doctors, business men, and landowners, and every literate person in the town, at home, office, and club. To some places, when he was hard-pressed for time, he sent Mohan.

§

In a few weeks he settled down to a routine. Every morning he left his bed at five o'clock and went to the station to meet the train from Madras at five-thirty. He took the bundles of papers and sent them in various directions with the cycle boys. After that he returned home, and went to his office only at eleven o'clock, and stayed there till five in the evening, when Mohan would drop in after posting his news for the day. Often Mohan would set him on the track of new clients : " I have reported an interesting criminal case to-day. Full details will appear in to-morrow's paper." As soon as the report appeared Chandran would go to the parties concerned and show them the news in print and induce them to part with a month's subscription, or if that was not possible, at least manage to sell them some loose copies containing their names. Some persons would be so pleased to see their names in print that they would buy even a dozen copies at a time. These stray sales accounted for, on an average, half a dozen copies every day. Mohan reported a wide variety of topics : excise raids, football matches, accidents, " smart " arrests by police sub-inspectors, suicides, murders, thefts, lectures in Albert College Union, and social events like anniversaries, tea parties, and farewell dinners.

§

The *D. M.* was responsible for taking him back to his old college after two years. Mohan had secured the Union and college orders. One of the boys came and told Chandran one day, suddenly, " Sir, the college clerk says that they won't want the paper from to-morrow."

" Why ? "

"I don't know, sir. They said the same thing in the Union too."

Chandran went to the college in person. The Union clerk recognized him and asked, "How are you, Mr. Chandran?"

"I say, my boy tells me that you have stopped the paper. Have you any idea why?"

"I don't know, sir. It is the President's order."

"Who is the President this year?"

"History Ragavachar," said the clerk.

He left the Union and went to the college, to the good old right wing, in which his Professor's room was situated. Ragavachar was holding a small class in his room, and Chandran went back to the Union to wait till the end of the hour. He sat in the gallery of the debating hall, and nobody took any notice of him. One or two boys stared at him and passed. He had been the Prime Mover in this very hall on a score of occasions; he had been the focus of attention. In those days, when he sat like this in the interim periods, how many people would gather round him, how they would all swagger about and shout as if they owned the place, and how they would throw pitying looks at strangers who sometimes came to look at the Union and moved about the place timidly. "Not one here that belonged to my set, all new faces, all absolute strangers. Probably these were High School boys when we were in the college. . . . Ramu, Ramu. How often have I come here looking for Ramu. If any class or lecture threatened to be boring Ramu would prefer to come away and spend his time reading a novel here or up in the reading-room. He had been quite a warm friend, but probably people changed. Time passed swiftly in Ramu's company. He would have some comment or other to make on every blessed thing on earth. . . . If he had real affection for a friend he should have written letters, especially when there was happy news like the securing of a job. Out of sight out of mind, but that is not a quality of friendship. There is no such thing as friendship. . . ."

Chandran rose from the gallery and stood looking at some group photos hanging on the wall. All your interests, joys, sorrows, hopes, contacts, and experience boiled down to group photos, Chandran thought. You lived in the college, thinking that you were the first and the last of your kind the college would ever see, and you ended as a group photo; the laughing, giggling fellows one saw about the Union now little knew that they would shortly be frozen into group photos. . . . He stopped before the group representing the 1931 set. He stood on tiptoe to see the faces. Many faces were familiar, but he could not recollect all their names. Where were all these now? He met so few of his classmates, though they had been two hundred strong for four years. Where were they? Scattered like spray. They were probably merchants, advocates, murderers, police inspectors, clerks, officers, and what not. Some must have gone to England, some married and had children, some turned agriculturists, dead and starving and unemployed, all at grips with life, like a buffalo caught in the coils of a python. . . .

There was Veeraswami, the revolutionary. He had appeared only once on the sands of Sarayu, like a dead man come to life for an instant. He had talked of some brigade and a revolution and Nature Cure. Where was he? What had he done with himself? . . . Among the people seated in the front row there was Natesan, the old Union Secretary, always in complications, always grumbling and arranging meetings. Chandran realized that he hadn't heard of Natesan after the examination; didn't know to which part of the country he belonged. He had been a good friend, very helpful and accommodating; but for his help the Historical Association could not have done any work. Where was he? Had he committed suicide? Could an advertisement be inserted in the papers: "Oh, Natesa, my friend, where are you?"

The bell rang. Chandran hurried out to meet Ragavachar. He saw several students walking in the corridors of the college. Scores of new faces. "At any rate they were better built in our days. All these fellows are puny." He recognized a few that had been the rawest juniors in his days, but were senior students now. They greeted him with smiles, and he felt greatly pleased. He strode into Ragavachar's room. Ragavachar sat in his chair and was just returning his spectacles to their case.

"Good-morning, sir," said Chandran. The Professor appeared to be slightly loose in the joints now. How he had been terrified of him in those days, Chandran reflected, as the Professor opened his case, put on the spectacles, and surveyed his visitor. There was no recognition in his manner.

"Please sit down," said the Professor, still trying to place his visitor.

"Don't you recognize me, sir?"

"Were you in this college at any time?"

"Yes, sir, in 1931. I was the first secretary of the Historical Association. My name is H. V. Chandran."

"H. V. Chandran," the Professor repeated reflectively. "Yes, yes. I remember. How are you ? What are you doing now ? You see, about two hundred persons pass out of the college every year ; sometimes it is difficult to recollect, you see."

Chandran had never thought that Ragavachar could talk so mildly. In those days how his voice silenced whole classes !

" What are you doing, Chandran ? "

Chandran told him, and then stated his business.

" Send for the Union clerk," said the Professor. When the clerk came, he asked, " Why have you stopped the *Daily Messenger* ? "

" There was a President's order to stop some of the papers," replied the clerk.

" And you chose the *Daily Messenger*, I suppose ? " growled Ragavachar. His voice had lost none of its tigerishness. " Which daily are you getting in the Union ? "

" The *Everyday Post*, sir."

This name set up a slight agitation in Chandran. The *Post* was his deadliest enemy ; but for it he would have enlisted a thousand subscribers in a fortnight. He said, " The *Post* ! It isn't served by the Planet News Service, sir."

" Isn't it ? " asked Ragavachar.

" No, sir. It gets only the ' C ' grade of the B. K. Press Agency."

"Is there much difference?"

"Absolutely, sir. I am not saying it because I am the agent of the *Messenger*. You can compare the telegrams in the *Messenger* with those in the *Post*, and you will see the difference, sir. B. K. Agency is not half as wide an organization as the Planet, and its 'C' grade is its very lowest service, and supplies the minimum news; the 'A' and 'B' grades are better. Our paper gets the 'A' and 'B' grades of the B. K. Agency in addition to the First Grade of the Planet Service; so that our paper gives all the news available."

"Still, a lot of people buy the *Post*," said Ragavachar.

"No, sir. Quite a lot of people are buying now only the *Messenger*. The circulation of the *Post* has steadily gone down to 2,000. Once upon a time it reigned supreme, when it was the only paper in the South."

Ragavachar turned to the clerk and commanded, "Get the *Messenger* from to-morrow. Stop the *Post*."

When Chandran rose to go, the Professor said, "I wish you luck. Please keep in touch with us. It ought to be easier for our students to remember us than for us to remember them. So don't forget."

"Certainly not, sir," Chandran said, resolving at that moment to visit his Professor at least once a week.

The college library clerk told him that Gajapathi was in charge of the college reading-room. Chandran went to the Common Room and sent his card in and waited, wondering if Gajapathi was going to resumed his attacks on Dowden and Bradley.

"Hallo, hallo, Chandran. It is ages since I saw you. What are you doing now?" Gajapathi put his arm round Chandran's shoulders and patted him. Chandran was taken aback by this affability, something they had not thought him capable of. Except for this Gajapathi had not changed. He still wore his discoloured frame spectacles and the drooping moustache.

When Chandran stated his business, Gajapathi said, "If they are getting the *Messenger* in the Union we can't get it in the college reading-room, because the Principal has passed an order that papers and magazines should not be duplicated in the two reading-rooms."

"But it is a waste of money to get the *Post*, sir. There is absolutely no news in it. It has a very inadequate service for telegrams, and it hasn't half as many correspondents as the *Messenger* has."

"Whatever it is, that is the Principal's order."

"Why don't you subscribe to my paper, sir?"

"Me! I never read any newspaper."

Chandran was horrified to hear it. "What do you do for news, sir?"

"I am not interested in any news."

Evidently this man read only Shakespeare and his critics.

"Well, sir, if you won't consider it a piece of impertinence, I think you ought to get into the newspaper habit. I am sure you will like it. I am sure you wouldn't like to be without it even for a day."

"Very well then, send it along. What is the subscription?"

"Two-eight a month and the paper is delivered at your door."

"Here it is, for a month." Gajapathi took out his purse and gave a month's subscription. "You can ask your boy to deliver it to me at——"

"Thank you, sir. I shall send the receipt tomorrow."

"Don't you trouble yourself about it. I only want my old students to do well in life. I am happy when I see it."

Chandran had never known this fact, and now he was profoundly moved by it.

" You must visit my office some time, sir," he said.

" Certainly, certainly. Where is it ? "

Before parting, Chandran tried to gratify him by saying, " I have been reading a lot since I left the college, sir."

" Really very glad to hear it. What have you been reading ? "

" A little of Shakespeare ; some Victorian essayists. But in fiction I think the present-day writers are really the masters. Don't you think, sir, that Wells, Galsworthy, and Hardy are superior to the old novelists ? "

Gajapathi paused before pronouncing an opinion. " I honestly think that there has not been anything worth reading after the eighteenth century, and for any one who cares for the real flavour of literature nothing to equal the Elizabethans. All the rest is trash."

" Galsworthy, sir ? "

" I find him tiresome."

" Wells and Hardy ? " gasped Chandran.

" Wells is a social thinker, hardly a literary figure. He is a bit cranky too. Hardy ? Much over-rated ; some parts of *Tess* good."

Chandran realized that Time had not touched his

fanaticisms. What an unknown, unsuspected enemy Wells, Galsworthy, Hardy, and a host of critics had in Gajapathi, Chandran thought.

"Don't forget to visit my office, sir, some time," Chandran pleaded before taking his leave.

CHAPTER SIXTEEN

ONE evening at five o'clock, as Chandran sat in his office signing receipts and putting them in envelopes for distribution next morning, his father walked in. Chandran pushed his chair back and rose, quite surprised, for Father seldom came to the office ; he had dropped in on the opening day, and again at another time with a friend, explaining apologetically that the friend wanted to see Chandran. Now this was his third visit.

" Sit down, Chandar, don't disturb yourself," said Father and tried to sit on the bench. Chandran pushed the chair towards him, entreating him to be seated on it.

Father looked about and asked, " How is your business ? "

" Quite steady, Father. The only trouble is in collection. If I go in person they pay the subscription ; if I send the boys they put them off with some excuse or other. I can't be visiting the 350 subscribers in person every morning. I must engage a bill collector. I can just afford one now."

" Are they pleased with your work in the Head Office ? "

" They must be. For six months I have shown a monthly average of over fifty new subscriptions ; but they have not written anything, which is a good sign. I don't expect anything better. If work is unsatisfactory our bosses will bark at us ; if it is satisfactory they won't say so, but merely keep quiet."

" You are right. In Government service too it is the same ; the best that we can expect from those above us is a very passive appreciation."

And then the conversation lagged for some time. Father suddenly said, " I have come on a mission. I was sent by your mother."

" Mother ? "

" Yes. She wants this thing to be made known to you. She is rather nervous to talk to you about it herself. So she has sent me."

" What is it, Father ? "

" But I wish you to understand clearly that I have not done anything behind your back. I have had no hand in this. It is entirely your mother's work."

" What is it, Father ? "

" You see, Mr. Jayarama Iyer, who is a leading lawyer in Talapur, sent his daughter's horoscope to us some time ago ; and for courtesy's sake yours was sent to them in return. Yesterday they have written to say that the horoscopes match very well, and asking if we have any objection to this alliance. I was for dropping the whole matter there, but your mother is very eager to make it known to you and to leave it to your decision. They have got in touch with us through our Ganapathi Sastrigal."

Chandran sat looking at the floor. His father paused for a moment and said, " I hear that the girl is about fifteen. They have sent a photo. She is good-looking. You can have a look at the photo if you like. They have written that she is very fair. They are prepared to give a cash dowry of 3,000 and other presents."

He waited for Chandran's answer. Chandran looked at him. There were drops of sweat on Father's brow, and his voice slightly quivered. Chandran felt a great pity for his father. What a strain this talk and the preparation for it must have been to him ! Father sat silent for a moment and then said, rising, " I will be going now. I have to go to the club."

Chandran saw his father off at the door and watched his back as he swung his cane and walked down the road. Chandran suddenly realized that he hadn't said anything in reply, and that his father might interpret silence for consent and live on false hopes. What a dreadful thing. He called his office boy, who was squatting on the steps of a neighbouring shop, asked him to remain in the office, took out his cycle, and pedalled in the direction his father had taken. Father hadn't gone far. Chandran caught up with him.

"You want me?"

"Yes, Father."

Father slowed down, and Chandran followed him, looking at the ground. "You have taken the trouble to come so far, Father, but I must tell you that I can't marry, Father."

"It is all right, Chandar. Don't let that bother you."

Chandran followed him for a few yards, and said, "Shall I go back to the office?"

"Yes."

As Chandran was about to mount his cycle, Father stopped him and said, "I saw in your office some papers and letters lying loose on your table. They are likely to be blown away by a wind. Remind me, I will give you some paperweights to-morrow."

He came back to his table and tried to sign a few more receipts. His father's visit opened a lid that had smothered raging flames. It started once again all the old controversies that racked one's soul. It violently shook a poise that was delicate and attained with infinite trouble and discipline.

He could not sign any more receipts. He pushed away the envelopes and the receipt books in order to make room for his elbows, which he rested on the table, and sat with his face in his hands, staring at the opposite wall.

Mohan came at six o'clock. He flung his cap on the table and sat down on the bench before the table, obstructing Chandran's view of the opposite wall.

Chandran asked mechanically, "What is the latest news?"

"Nothing special. The usual drab nonsense; lectures and sports and suicides. I am seriously thinking of resigning."

He was very sullen.

"What is wrong now?" asked Chandran.

"Everything. I took up this work as a stop-gap till I should get a footing in the literary world. And now what has happened? Reporting has swallowed me up. From morning to night I roam about the town, noting other people's business, and then go back to the hotel and sleep. I hardly have any inclination to write a single line of poetry. It is four months since I wrote a single line. The stuff you see in the magazine page are my old bits. When I take my pen I can't write anything more soul-stirring than 'Judgment was delivered to-day in a case in which somebody or other stood charged with something or other. . . .'"

"I am very hungry," said Chandran. "Shall we go to a hotel?"

"Yes."

When they came out of the hotel, Mohan's mood had changed. He now condemned his previous mood. "If I have not written anything, it is hardly anybody's fault. I ought to plan my time to include it."

They smoked a few cigarettes and walked along the river. They walked to Nallappa's Grove, crossed over to the opposite bank, walked some distance there, turned back, and sat down on the sands. Mohan went on talking and solacing himself by planning. He even stretched the definition of poetry; he said that there ought to be no special thing called poetry, and that if one was properly constituted one ought to get a poetic thrill out of the composing of even news paragraphs. There ought to be no narrow boundaries. There ought to be a proper synthesis of life.

When Mohan had exhausted his poetic theories, Chandran quietly said, " My father came to the office at five o'clock with an offer of marriage." The troubles of a poet instantly ceased or were forgotten. He listened in silence to Chandran's narration of his father's visit. And Mohan dared not comment. From the manner in which Chandran spoke Mohan couldn't tell which way he was inclined ; there was the usual denunciation of Love, Marriage, and Woman, but at the same time there was a lack of fire in the denunciation. Mohan could not decide whether it was the beginning of a change of attitude or whether it was a state of atrophy, so complete that even fury and fire were dead. Chandran concluded, " . . . And I ran after my father and told him that it was unthinkable."

Chandran stopped. Mohan did not offer any comment. For some moments there was only the rustle of the banyan branches on the water's edge.

" I am very sorry for my poor mother, for her wild hope and her fears. I curse myself for having brought her to this state. But what can I do ? What other answer could I give to my father ? "

" How did he take it ? "

" Quite indifferently. He talked of paperweights. My trouble is, I don't know, I don't know. I can't get angry with my mother for busying herself with my marriage again. I have had enough of it once."

"Then leave it alone. You are under no compulsion to worry about it."

"But I pity my father and mother. What a frantic attempt. There is something in the whole business that looks very pathetic to me."

"What I can't understand is," said Mohan, "why you are still worrying about it, seeing that you have very politely told your father that it is unthinkable. I can't understand why you still talk about it."

"You are right. That question is settled. Let us talk of something else."

"Something else" was not easy to find. There was another interlude of silence.

"Shall we be starting back?" asked Mohan.

"Yes," said Chandran, but again sat in silence, not making any effort to get up. For nearly a quarter of an hour Mohan sat listening to the voice of the river, and Chandran drew circles in the sand.

"What would you do in my place?" asked Chandran abruptly.

"How can I say? What would you do in mine?" asked Mohan.

Chandran asked directly, "What would you honestly advise me to do ?"

"If the girl is not bad-looking, and if you are getting some money into the bargain, why don't you marry ? You will have some money and the benefits of a permanent help-mate."

Chandran remarked that Mohan had grown very coarse and prosaic. No wonder he could not write any more poetry.

Stung by this Mohan said, "If one has to marry one must do it for love, if there is such a thing, or for the money and comforts. There is no sense in shutting your eyes to the reality of things. I am beginning to believe in a callous realism." He liked immensely the expression he had invented. He loved it. He delivered a short speech on Callous Realism. He had not thought of it till now. Now that he had coined the expression he began to believe in it fully. He raised it to the status of a personal philosophy. Before he had expatiated for five minutes on it, he became a fanatic. He challenged all other philosophies, and pleaded for more Callous Realism in all human thought. When he reached the height of intoxication, he said with a great deal of callous realism, "I don't see why you shouldn't consider this offer with the greatest care and attention. You get a fat three thousand, and get a good-looking companion, who will sew on your buttons, mend your clothes, and dust your furniture while you are out distributing newspapers, and who will bring the coffee to your room. In addition to all this, it is always pleasant to have a soft companion near at hand."

" And on top of it pleasing one's parents," added Chandran.

" Quite right. Three cheers for Her Majesty the Soft Companion," cried Mohan.

" Hip, hip, hooray ! "

The callous realist now asked, " Will you kindly answer a few questions I am going to ask ? "

" Yes."

" You must answer my questions honestly and truthfully. They are to search your heart."

" Right, go on," said Chandran.

" Are you still thinking of Malathi ? "

" I have trained my mind not to. She is another man's wife now."

" Do you love the memory of her still ? "

" I don't believe in love. It doesn't exist in my philosophy. There is no such thing as love. If I am not unkind to my parents it is because of gratitude, and nothing else. If I get a wife I shall not wrench her hand or swear at her, because it would be indecent. That is all the motive for a lot of habitual decent behaviour we see, which we call love. There is no such thing as love."

"Then it ought not to make any difference to you whether you marry or not; and so why don't you marry when you know that it will please your parents, when you are getting a lot of money, and when you are earning so well?"

There was no answer to this. Chandran chewed these thoughts in silence, and then said, "Mohan, let us toss and decide." They rose and walked across the sand to a dim municipal lantern at the end of North Street. The lantern threw a pale yellow circle of light around a central shadow. Chandran took a copper coin from his pocket. Mohan held Chandran's hand and said, "Put that back. Let us toss a silver coin. Marriage, you know." Mohan took out a four-anna silver coin, balanced it on the forefinger of his right hand, and asked, "Shall I toss?"

"Yes. Heads, marriage."

"Right."

Mohan tossed the silver coin. It fell down in the dim circumference of light. Both stooped. Mohan shouted, "You must keep your word. Heads. Ha! Ha!"

"Is it?" There was a tremor in Chandran's voice. "Very well, if the girl is good-looking, only if she is good-looking," said Chandran.

"That goes without saying," said Mohan, picking up the coin and putting it in his pocket.

CHAPTER SEVENTEEN

EARLY in the morning, five days later, Chandran, with his mother, was in a train going to Talapur. He was to look at the girl who had been proposed to him, and then give his final word.

He said to his mother for the dozenth time, " If I don't like the girl, I hope they won't mind."

" Not at all. Before I married your father, some three or four persons came and looked at me and went away."

" Why did they not approve of you ? " Chandran asked, looking at her.

" It is all a matter of fate," said Mother. " You can marry only the person whom you are destined to marry and at the appointed time. When the time comes, let her be the ugliest girl, she will look all right to the destined eye."

" None of that. Mother," Chandran protested. " I won't marry an ugly girl."

" Ugliness and beauty is all as it strikes one's eye. Every one has his own vision. How do all the ugly girls in the world get married ? "

Chandran became apprehensive. " Mother, are you suggesting that this girl is ugly ? "

" Not at all. Not at all. See her for yourself and decide. You have the photo."

" She is all right in the photo, but that may be only a trick of the camera."

" You will have to wait for only a few hours more. You can see her and then give your decision."

" But, Mother, to go all the way to their house and see the girl, and then to say we can't marry her. That won't be nice."

" What is there in it ? It is the custom. When a girl is ready for marriage her horoscope will be sent in ten directions, and ten different persons will see her and approve or disapprove, or they might be disapproved by the girl herself ; and after all only one will marry her. A year before my marriage a certain doctor was eager for an alliance with our family ; the horoscopes, too, matched ; and his son came to look at me, but I didn't like his appearance, and told my father that I wouldn't marry him. It was after that that your father was proposed, and he liked my appearance, and when my father asked me if I would marry him I didn't say ' no.' It is all settled already, the husband of every girl and wife of every man. It is in nobody's choice."

They reached Talapur at 4 p.m. A boy of about eighteen came and peeped into the compartment and asked, " Are you from Malgudi ? "

" Yes," said Chandran.

" I am Mr. Jayarama Iyer's son. Shall I ask my servant to carry your baggage ? "

" We have brought nothing. We are going back by the seven o'clock train, you see," said Chandran. Chandran and his mother exchanged a brief look. " This is the girl's brother," the look said. Chandran took another look at the boy and tried to guess the appearance of the girl. If the girl looked anything like her brother. . . ! The boy was dark and rugged. Probably this was not her own brother ; he might be her first cousin. Chandran opened his mouth, and was about to ask if Jayarama Iyer was his own father, but he checked himself and asked instead, " Are you Mr. Jayarama Iyer's eldest son ? "

" I am his second son," replied the boy. This answer did not throw any light on the appearance of the girl, as, in some absurd manner, Chandran had imagined that it would.

The boy took them to a car outside. They were soon in the Extensions.

They were welcomed into the house by Mr. Jayarama Iyer and his wife, both of whom subjected

Chandran to a covert examination just as he tried to make out something of his future relatives-in-law. He found Mr. Jayarama Iyer to be a middle-aged person with a greying crop and a sensitive face. He was rather dark, but Chandran noted that the mother looked quite fair, and hoped that the girl would have a judicious mixture of the father's sensitive appearance and the mother's complexion.

And to his immense satisfaction he found that it was so, when, about an hour later, she appeared before him. She had to be coaxed and cajoled by her parents to come to the hall. With her eyes fixed on the ground she stepped from an inner room, a few inches into the hall, trembling and uncertain, ready to vanish in a moment.

Chandran's first impulse was to look away from the girl. He spent a few seconds looking at a picture on the wall; but suddenly remembered that he simply could not afford to look at anything else now. With a sudden decision, he turned his head and stared at her. She was dressed in a blue sari. A few diamonds glittered in her ear-lobes and neck. His heart gave a wild beat and, as he thought, stopped. "Her figure is wonderful," some corner of his mind murmured. "Her face must also be wonderful, but I can't see it very well, she is looking at the ground." Could he shriek out to Mr. Jayarama Iyer, sitting in the chair on his right and uttering inanities at this holy moment, "Please ask your daughter to look up, sir. I can't see her face?"

Mr. Jayarama Iyer said to his daughter, "You mustn't be so shy, my girl. Come here. Come here."

The girl was still hesitating and very nervous. Chandran felt a great sympathy for her. He pleaded, "Sir, please don't trouble her. Let her stay there."

"As you please," said Jayarama Iyer.

At this moment the girl slightly raised her head and stole a glance at Chandran. He saw her face now. It was divine; there was no doubt about it. He secretly compared it with Malathi's, and wondered what he had seen in the latter to drive him so mad....

Jayarama Iyer said to his daughter, "Will you play a little song on the *veena*?" Chandran saw that she was still nervous, and once again rushed to her succour. "Please don't trouble her, sir. I don't mind. She seems to be nervous."

"She is not nervous," said the father. "She plays very well, and also sings."

"I am happy to hear that, sir, but it must be very difficult for her to sing now. I hope to hear her music some other day."

Jayarama Iyer looked at him with amusement and said, "All right."

It was with a very heavy heart that Chandran allowed himself to be carried away in the car from the bungalow. He could have cried when he said, "Good-bye" to his future brother-in-law, and the train moved out of Talapur station.

His mother asked him in the train, "Do you like the girl?"

"Yes, Mother," said Chandran with fervour. "Did you tell them that?"

"We can't tell them anything till they come and ask us."

Chandran made a gesture of despair and said, "Oh, these formalities. I loathe them. All this means unnecessary delay. Why shouldn't we send them a wire to-morrow?"

"Be patient. Be patient. All in its time, Chandra."

"But supposing they don't ask us?"

"They will. In two or three days they will come to us or write."

"I ought to have told Mr. Jayarama Iyer that I liked his girl," Chandran said regretfully.

Mother asked apprehensively, "I hope you have not done any such thing?"

" No, Mother."

" Patience, Chandra. You must allow things to be done in proper order."

Chandran leaned back, resigned himself to his fate, and sat looking out of the window sulkily.

He asked, " Mother, do you like the girl ? "

" Yes, she is good-looking."

" Is her voice all right ? Does she talk all right ? "

" She talks quite well."

" Does she talk intelligently ? "

" Oh, yes. But she spoke very little before me. She was shy before her future mother-in-law."

" What class is she reading in, Mother ? "

" Sixth Form."

" Is she a good student ? "

" Her mother says that she is very good in her class."

" Her father says that she plays very well on the *veena*. It seems she can also sing very well. . . . Mother, her name is ? " He knew it very well, but loved to hear it again.

" Susila," Mother said.

" I know it," Chandran said, fearing that his Mother might understand him. " I want to know if she has any other name at home."

" Her mother called her once or twice before me, and she called her Susila."

For the rest of the journey the music of the word " Susila " rang in his ears. Susila, Susila, Susila. Her name, music, figure, face, and everything about her was divine. Susila, Susila—Malathi, not a spot beside Susila ; it was a tongue-twister ; he wondered why people liked that name.

CHAPTER EIGHTEEN

§

A FORTNIGHT later the ceremony of the Wedding Notice was celebrated. Jayarama Iyer and a party came to Malgudi for that purpose. It was a day of feast and reception in Chandran's house. A large number of guests were invited, and at the auspicious moment Jayarama Iyer stood up and read the saffron-touched paper which announced that, by the blessing of God, Chandran, son of so and so, was to marry Susila, daughter of so and so, on a particular auspicious date, ten days hence.

The days that followed were days of intense activity. They were days of preparation for the wedding, a period in which Chandran felt the *Daily Messenger* a great nuisance. Chandran had an endless round of visits to make every day, to the tailor, to the jewellers, to the silk shops, and to the printer.

The invitation cards, gold-edged and elegantly printed, were sent to over a thousand in Malgudi and outside. It was while sitting in his office and writing down the addresses that Chandran realized once again how far time had removed him from old classmates and friends. He was very anxious not to miss any one. But with the utmost difficulty he could remember only a dozen or so that he occasionally met in the town ; he could recollect a few more, but couldn't trace their whereabouts. It rent his heart when he realized his helplessness in regard to even Ramu, Veeraswami, and Natesan. While he knew that Ramu was somewhere in Bombay, there was no one who could give him his address. Heaven knew where Natesan was. And Veeraswami ? " Probably he is a political prisoner somewhere, or he may be in Russia now."

" Or it is more likely that he is a tame clerk in some Government office," said Mohan.

" What has happened to his Brigade ? "

" I have no idea ; he came to my hotel once or twice some years ago. I didn't see him after that."

" Probably his brigade has a strength of a million members now, all of whom may be waiting to overthrow the Government," said Chandran.

"It is more likely that he has a lucrative job as a police informer," said the cynical poet. He repeated, "I have no idea where he is. He came and stayed in my hotel twice several months or years ago."

This started a train of memories in Chandran. Evenings and evenings ago; Chandran, Mohan and Veeraswami, Malathi evenings; mad days. . . . There was a radiance about Susila that was lacking in Malathi. . . . No, no. He checked himself this time; he told himself that it was very unfair to compare and decry; it was a very vile thing to do. He told himself that he was doing it only out of spite. . . . Poor Malathi! For the first time he was able to view her as a sister in a distant town. Poor girl, she had her points. Of course Susila was different.

"What are you thinking?" asked Mohan.

"That postmaster, the Maduram postmaster, we must send him a card. I don't know if he still remembers me."

§

While Chandran was away at Talapur for his wedding, Mohan looked after the newspaper.

Chandran returned a new man, his mind full of

Susila, the fragrance of jasmine and sandal paste, the smokiness of the Sacred Fire, of brilliant lights, music, gaiety, and laughter.

For nearly a month after that Mohan had to endure monologues from Chandran: "On the first day she was too shy to talk to me. It was only on the third day that she uttered a few syllables. Before I came away she spoke quite a lot. Shy at first, you know. She is a very sensible girl; talks very intelligently. I asked her what she thought of me; she merely threw at me a mischievous side-glance. She has a very mischievous look. She has promised to write to me on alternate days; she writes beautiful English. . . ."

Thereafter, every day, Chandran spent a large portion of his waking hours in writing letters to her or in receiving her letters. He would have to live on them for nearly a year more. His talks to Mohan were usually on the subject of these letters. "She has written a wonderful letter to me to-day, has addressed me as 'My Own Darling' for the first time; she has sent me twenty thousand kisses though I sent her only fifteen thousand in my last letter. . . ." Or "She likes very much the silk pieces that I sent to her. She says that they are wonderful." Or, touching his inner pocket, in which more than one of her letters always rested, " Poor girl ! She writes asking me to take very great care of my health. Says that I ought not to get up so early every morning. She has inquired about the business and wishes me more subscribers. She wishes the *Daily Messenger* long life and health. She has a very great sense of humour."

§

Two months later, one evening, Chandran was sitting in his office in a very depressed state. Mohan came, sat on the bench, and asked, " What is wrong ? "

Chandran lifted a careworn face to him, and said, " No letter even to-day. This is the sixth day. I don't know what the matter is."

" Probably she is studying for the examination or something. She will probably write to you to-morrow."

" I don't think so," said Chandran. He was in complete despair. " This is the first time she has not written for so many days."

Mohan was baffled. He had never been face to face with such a problem before.

Chandran said, " I shouldn't worry but for the fact that she is unwell. She wrote in her last letter that she had a bad cold. She is probably down with high fever now. Who knows what fever it might be."

"It may be just malaria," hazarded Mohan.

"For six days, unintermittently!" Chandran laughed gloomily. "I dare not name anything now. I don't know if her people will attend to her properly. . . . I must go in person and see. I shall go home now, and then catch the six o'clock train. I shall be in Talapur to-morrow morning. Till I come back, please look after the office, will you?"

"Yes," said Mohan to the afflicted man.

"Many thanks. I shall try to be back soon," said Chandran and rose. He stepped into the road, took out his cycle from its stand, and said to Mohan, "I have marked two addresses on the tablet. If they don't give the subscription tell the boys not to deliver them the papers to-morrow."

As he was ready to get on the cycle, Mohan ran to the door, and said, "Look here, not that I shirk work and don't want to look after the office or anything, but why do you suppose all these terrible things? On the authority of absent letters and the mention of a slight cold?"

Chandran scorned this question, jumped on his

cycle without a word, and pedalled away. Mohan stood looking after the cycle for some time, and turned in, throwing up his arms in despair. But then, it is a poet's business only to ask questions ; he cannot always expect an answer.